10664555

# Coal Country Ghosts

# Legends and Lore

## Schuylkill and Carbon Counties, Pennsylvania

## Charles J. Adams III

### EXETER HOUSE BOOKS

# Coal Country Ghosts, Legends, and Lore

©2004  Charles J. Adams III

All rights reserved under the U.S. Copyright Law.
No portion of this book may be reproduced
in any form whatsoever, except with written
permission from the publisher.

For information, contact:
**EXETER HOUSE BOOKS**
P.O. Box 8134
Reading, PA 19603
www.ExeterHouseBooks.com

FIRST EDITION 2004
PRINTED IN THE UNITED STATES OF AMERICA

ISBN 1-880683-20-2

*To Maddie, who departed...*
*...and Alanna, who arrived.*

# TABLE OF CONTENTS

# ACKNOWLEDGMENTS

## Societies, Organizations

The Historical Society of Schuylkill County, Mauch Chunk Historical Society of Carbon County, Summit Hill Historical Society, The Delaware & Lehigh National Heritage Corridor and State Heritage Park, Schuylkill County Visitors Bureau, Pocono Mountains Vacation Bureau, Mauch Chunk Museum, Philadelphia Ghost Hunters Alliance, Berks County Paranormal Association, Lehigh Valley Ghost Hunters, Pine Grove Historical Society, Cressona Historical Society, Schuylkill County Council for the Arts

## Books, Papers, Articles

"Black Rock: Mining Folklore of the Pennsylvania Dutch" George Kolson, Johns Hopkins Press, Baltimore, 1960; "Lament for the Molly Maguires," Arthur H. Lewis; Harcourt, Brace, 1964; "Mysteries on the Mountain," David A. Wargo, Black Diamond Entertainment Co., 2002; Publications of the Schuylkill County Historical Society; "Old Schuylkill Tales," Ella Zerbey Elliott; "Powowwing: A Persistent American Esoteric Tradition," David W. Kriebel, Ph.D.; "The Realness of Witchcraft in America," A. Monroe Aurand, Jr., The Aurand Press, 1942; "History of Schuylkill County, Pa.," W.W. Munsell and Co., publishers, 1882; "The Mollie Maguires: The Origin, Growth and Character of the Organization," F.P. Dewees, 1877

## Newspapers, Magazines

The Times News, Shenandoah Herald, Pottsville Lantern, Allentown Morning Call, Pottsville Republican, Pottsville Journal, Philadelphia Times, Philadelphia Inquirer, Philadelphia Evening Bulletin, National Enquirer, Schuylkill Saturday, The News-Item, Schuylkill County Sampler, Pennsylvania Folklife, Panorama Anthracite, Schuylkill Haven Call, Keystone Folklore Quarterly, Mahanoy City Record-American, True Detective Mysteries, Reading Eagle, Reading Times, The Valley Gazette

## Individuals

Trooper Ray Albert, Pennsylvania State Police; Evelyn Hunsicker, Marigrace Heyer, Chuck Barr, Chuck Gallagher, Deborah Miller, Kim Cool, Ron Dalton...and many others who helped along the way but whose names were not recorded.

## Publisher and Research Assistant

# David J. Seibold

Charles J. Adams III (that's him at lower left, with a friend in Amsterdam, Holland) is a native of Reading, Pennsylvania. He has written more than 25 books on ghosts, hauntings, legends, shipwrecks, and train wrecks in Pennsylvania, New Jersey, New York, and Delaware. He has led "ghost tours" in New York City, Philadelphia, Scotland, Wales, and England, and has been featured on the History Channel, A&E, TLC, MTV, and the Travel Channel as a commentator and consultant on programs dealing with hauntings. An accomplished musician and songwriter, Adams is former president of the Reading Public Library, and has been on the board of directors of the Historical Society of Berks County for more than 25 years. In addition to his books, Adams also writes travel features for the Reading Eagle and is the morning personality on radio station WEEU, 830AM, in Reading.

Folk art is, indeed, the oldest of the aristocracies of thought, and because it refuses what is passing and trivial, the merely clever and pretty, it is the soil where all great art is rooted. In a society that has cast out imaginative tradition, only a few people–three or four thousand out of millions–favoured by their own characters and by happy circumstances, and only then after much labour, have understanding of imaginative things...and yet, the imagination is the man himself. And so, it has always seemed to me that we, who would re-awaken imaginative tradition by making old songs live again, or by gathering old stories into books, take part in the quarrel of Galilee.

W.B. Yeats
*Twilight of the Celts*
1901

# Coal Country Ghosts, Legends, and Lore

# INTRODUCTION
### by Rick Bugera
*Founder: Berks County Paranormal Association*
*Cofounder: Pennsylvania Paranormal Alliance*

Many people wonder why I have a fascination with the coal regions. After all, I'm from "down the line" in Berks County.

One of the main reasons I am interested in the coal regions is my heritage. My father's parents were Eastern European immigrants just like most of the people who labored in the mines. My grandparents had many friends that lived and worked in the coal regions and when they could find the time they went "up the line" to spend time with them and their families. When I was a child, my father would tell me stories about the coal regions and how he would go up there with his parents.

Sometimes we would take Sunday drives up through Schuylkill County into Carbon County and he would show me where his parents' friends had lived, where he would play when he went up there etc., etc.

Unfortunately my father passed away when I was sixteen years old and the trips to the coal regions came to an end. Although the trips to the coal regions stopped my fascination with the area was only starting to grow. As I grew older I started making my own trips up the line. I started making friends up there and started to learn even more about the history of the area.

There was one fascination that I harbor that is just as intense as my fascination for the coal regions–ghosts!

I developed that particular fascination at an early age after witnessing my first apparition. It didn't take long before I was heading out to supposedly haunted locations around my area in hopes of catching a glimpse of a ghost.

Before long I had heard about a book that was in the stores called *Ghost Stories of Berks County*

# Coal Country Ghosts, Legends, and Lore

by Charles J. Adams III. I knew the name Charlie Adams well, as my father used to listen to him on the morning show on Reading radio station WEEU, 830 AM. I took some of the money I had earned by delivering the Kutztown Patriot newspaper and I bought the book.

Well, I was hooked. Not only did the stories Charlie wrote enthrall me they also gave me a bunch of new places to go looking for ghosts. I spent quite a bit of time sitting in locations waiting and watching for ghosts, sometimes I experienced things that one would definitely have to say was a specter at work but most of the time I didn't see or experience anything.

It wasn't until the early 1990s that I discovered there was more to ghost hunting than sitting and waiting to see a ghost...much more! It was then that I started looking at ghosts from a more scientific standpoint.

Unfortunately at that point in time the internet was in its infancy and the number of people I knew that thought I was just plain nuts for what I was doing far out numbered those that had the same beliefs as mine. I stumbled through the next several years using very simple devices in order to try to come up with an explanation for these things we call ghosts and why they are here.

Around 1999 is when I finally got the

internet. I found several web sites that dealt with ghosts and ghost hunting. The internet also gave me access to several things that were in short demand before I logged on for the first time–like-minded people and much more sophisticated equipment.

I started purchasing some of the basics, an EMF meter to measure electromagnetic fields, a cheap 35mm camera to attempt to capture a ghost on film, and a digital thermometer to measure those cold spots that we all have heard about.

It didn't take me long to head out to some of the locations that I had spent countless hours sitting at and seeing nothing. It didn't take much longer before I got a roll of film developed and there it was–smoke-like mist coming out of a tombstone!

I went back to that particular cemetery with my basic equipment and low and behold I got an EMF reading at that same tombstone! I had my first piece of evidence that ghosts just might exist. It wasn't too long after that happened that a close friend of mine shared an interesting but rather personal experience he had had with what he believed might have been the ghost of his recently departed mother.

My friend had always been a nonbeliever in ghosts so hearing this story come from him made it all the more credible to me. I talked to him at length about ghosts and what I believed they might be and within several weeks my friend started joining me on my little ghost hunts.

That was the beginning of what is now the Berks County Paranormal Association or BCPA for short. The BCPA is a group that is dedicated to finding decisive evidence of the existence of ghosts through scientific means.

The basic equipment has long since been replaced by much more sophisticated and costly gear but our intentions and motivations are still the same as they were when I first started doing this around twenty years ago.

Although we use the name Berks County in our title we do not limit ourselves to the boundaries of Berks. It is not uncommon for us to head up the line into the coal regions to do some research or investigate an alleged haunting.

Through my personal experiences I have found that the coal regions are as ripe with old legends and lore as it is with history. History breeds legend. Without history there would be no ghost stories for us to investigate, no legends for us to tell next to a crackling campfire late at night, and no lore for us to pass down to our descendants.

Some of the stories you will be reading in this

book are actual eyewitness accounts of ghostly activity, others are stories that have been passed down from generation to generation, and still others will be what we call urban legend. An urban legend is a story that usually appears mysteriously and spreads spontaneously in various forms. Sometimes there is a hint of truth to the story but not always. A good example of an urban legend is that mixing Pop Rocks candy and cola will have a fatal effect on a person. Most people have heard this story but is there any truth to it? No. It is perfectly safe to consume those two items at the same time. Urban legends spread like wildfire. Many times they involve ghosts, escaped mental patients that have a lust for blood, or involve popular establishments that everyone has heard of.

This book is long overdue. Hopefully it will not only entertain you but will also educate you a bit about the history that surrounds you.

Maybe you will be reading this book for the first time and realize what I realized around 1984–Charlie Adams is not just a good writer, his books are a great source of information for the ghost enthusiast. Please enjoy this book and pass along the stories to your children so they can do the same with their children.

# The Broad Mountain Ghost

On Palm Sunday, April 25, 1925. Claude and Mary Duncan were hiking a short distance off the main road over Broad Mountain between Heckscherville and Gordon, searching for May flowers in the deep woods.

They would make a discovery that horrified them and touch off one of the most sensational crime stories in Schuylkill County history.

And although they could not have known then, what they found was also the genesis for what is certainly the most sensational ghost story in the county.

7

# Coal Country Ghosts, Legends, and Lore

Ask anyone anywhere in Coal Country if they know any ghost stories, and they will readily recall the "Broad Mountain (or, to some, the Gordon Mountain) Ghost."

Broad Mountain is the topographic backbone, and to some extent the demographic divider of Schuylkill County. It is also the incubator of many legends and tales.

On that Sunday in 1925, those two individuals walking on an old logging road were distracted by a cawing flock of crows that circled incessantly over a clearing in the woods. They headed for that spot and came upon a most grisly scene.

A portion of grass had been charred by a fire, and in the middle of it was the mutilated, badly-burned corpse of a young woman. Her skull was fractured, her face was twisted in a painful grimace. There were gashes on her arm and scalp. She had met a most horrible fate.

An investigation into the murder resolved little. It was believed that the girl was between 16 and 20 years old, and that she might have been bludgeoned somewhere else and taken to Broad Mountain where the killer administered the *coup de grace* by setting her body afire. A rainfall later in the day likely doused the fire and left her body partially-burned.

Some local folks speculated that the girl might

have been a "lady" who worked at the Sunset Inn, a well-known brothel in Numidia, or perhaps a runaway from a local institution. An intensive probe ensued, but yielded nothing. The girl's murder is yet to be solved.

A bizarre twist to the story unfolded following an autopsy that was performed on the body. In hopes that someone might someday emerge and identify the girl, her head was severed and preserved in an Ashland doctor's office for 17 years before being removed to the Pennsylvania State Police headquarters in Harrisburg. A plaster cast was made of the head, and that has since found its way into a storage area of the Historical Society of Schuylkill County.

Almost the very next night after the body was removed, rumors began to circulate that the poor girl's ghost remained on Broad Mountain, searching through eternity for her killer.

To this day, it is said that a misty figure floats over and around the site of "Jane Doe's" murder. The energy of the slain girl is so strong that it can dim the headlights of cars as they pass over Broad Mountain and, if conditions are just right (or wrong, depending on your outlook), that energy can actually shut down a car's engine.

In stories told over the years, the girl's ghost is most often described as being a translucent white, gliding in aimless and endless circles throughout the forests between Gordon and Heckscherville.

Reports of and reaction to the Broad Mountain Ghost reached the point of near hysteria at some points in time. Veritable traffic jams were not uncommon on the mountain road on the anniversary of the murder and at Halloween in the years immediately following the heinous homicide.

Groups of "ghost hunters" would gather at the murder site and conduct seances in hopes of conjuring up the girl's spirit. Others would go there to pray that her restless spirit find peace.

To this day, the murder is an unsolved "cold case" and the ghost story remains forever in the annals of Coal Country folklore.

## THE GREAT GHOSTLY HOAX

In 1973, former Gordon auto dealer J.A. Seitzinger revealed that he and two friends had contributed greatly to the earliest rampant rumors of spirit spottings on Broad Mountain just after the murder of the young woman. The trio set up an elaborate display of dangling mannequins and bed sheets. In what he boasted as "the only time the true story (of the ghost) has been told," Seitzinger wrote in the *Evening Herald* that after so many people had so many experiences on the mountain, "I considered it our civic duty to see that these visitors would see a ghost." Interestingly, Seitzinger did not dismiss the possibility that there really was a ghost on the mountain. In his revelation, he noted: "I understand ghosts do not grow old or die like humans, so it probably will be around a long time after I have passed on."

**10**

# The Eternal Hunter

Stories of "The Eternal Hunter," or, as the early German settlers called him *Der Ewich Yaeger*, are repeated in folk tales told throughout several counties in eastern Pennsylvania.

In Schuylkill County, pharmacist J. Hampton Haldeman told of the hunter who stands an endless vigil in the mountains near Pine Grove.

*It's an old story that dates back 200 years. It seems that at that time the summer had been very, very dry. The creeks were practically waterless. The crops failed, and naturally, the game–deer and rabbits–crossed over the mountain; that is, the other side of these Blue Mountains. The villagers were in dire circumstances. Venison was a cheap source of food. One of the old men decided that he would take his dogs, go across the mountain, and chase back the deer to save the community of Pine Grove. When he left he said he would hunt forever, if necessary, even through the sky, to chase the deer back.*

*And that is one reason why late at night in the fall you hear noises in the sky, the sounds of barking, and the report of shotgun fire. It is ghost of the Ewich Yaeger. He's hunting forever through the sky.*

**11**

*...from an old newspaper account of...*

# The Legend of Regina Hartman

What follows is neither a ghost story nor does it take place entirely in the "Coal Country" of Pennsylvania. Yet, it is an enduring and endearing saga that warrants inclusion in this volume of legends and lore from the heart of the Blue Mountains.

It is what has been called "the romantic tale"

of a little girl named Regina.

The setting was a humble homestead in the deep forest of southern Schuylkill County. The year was 1755. Tensions were high between the pioneers who were moving into the region and the natives who had been incited by the French to believe that the English and German settlers were their enemies.

John and Magdalena Hartman had come to America from Reutlingen, Germany, and had made their first home just west of Reading. Soon, the couple and their children–George, Barbara, Christian, and Regina–resettled just north of the Schuylkill River Gap near what is now **Orwigsburg**.

There, with their dog, Wasser, they carved out a humble existence. As an 1897 recounting of the story noted, however: "In the very nature of things John Hartman could not have known that he was living on a volcano, as it were, whose eruption was close at hand, and whose destructive force must sweep him from the face of the earth."

It was a morning on a day in early autumn, 1755, when Magdalena Hartman and her son, Christian, left the home to purchase flour at a mill near Schuylkill Haven. John and his three other children remained home and tended to chores around the house.

But, shortly after Mrs. Hartman and her son departed, Wasser began to growl. The growl amplified into a barking frenzy and before anyone could mount any kind of defense, a band of Indians swooped down on the cabin.

John Hartman went for his rifle, but he and George were savagely attacked. One story printed in the *Reading Eagle* newspaper provided graphic details.

"A bullet sped through John Hartman's head, and another through his heart and he fell a lifeless corpse on his own threshold. His son, scarcely realizing what it all meant, rushed to aid his father, but the cleaving tomahawks sped through his brain and he sank down on the body of his dead father. The faithful 'Wasser' was seized and dispatched, and the little girls stood, chilled to the very soul with horror, alone."

The terror continued. The attackers grabbed ten year-old Barbara and nine year-old Regina and forced them to watch as they set their cabin and the bodies of their father, brother, and Wasser aflame.

In states of severe shock, the girls were captured by the Indians and as their home and loved ones were incinerated, they were taken on a long journey north, deep into New York state and the heartland of the natives.

As Barbara and Regina were spirited away by their captors, Magdalena and her son were making their way back home from the mill. Nothing could have prepared them for what they would find.

"When in sight of the farm, after emerging from the forest," the story reported, "the quick eye of young Christian, after gazing over the landscape, soon saw the change and his question, 'Why, mother, where is our house?' brought upon the poor woman a full realization of what had occurred, and before her lay the smoking ruins of her once happy home. The evidences of the disposition of her husband and son were soon disclosed. But where, oh where, were her poor helpless little girls?"

The survivors' grief was unimaginable. Mother and son had to live with the reality that their father and brother were gone, and Barbara and Regina were also, in all likelihood, dead.

Over the ensuing months, neighbors helped Magdalena and Christian rebuild the farm. In early spring, 1756, hunters discovered the decomposed remains of Barbara Hartman to the side of an Indian path in the Catawissa Valley. A tomahawk had been driven into her skull.

Magdalena had almost resigned herself to the probability that she would never see Regina again.

But, in 1764, word reached her that what had become known as the French and Indian War had ended, and hundreds of whites who had been kidnapped by the Indians and taken into their villages would be released to their families, if positive identification could be made.

Regina Hartman would have been in her late teens. Was there a chance she survived her capture and could be reunited with her mother and brother? It was worth a trip to Carlisle, Pennsylvania, to find out.

Upon arrival at the captives' camp, a tearful but hopeful Magdalena strolled slowly past lines of young women who had been taken from their homes and raised in the Indian ways. After several passes and several hours, all hope seemed lost. A compassionate Col. Henry Bouquet, who had arranged the reunion attempt, urged her to remember something–a phrase, a song, a hymn–that might stir old memories in her daughter's mind.

All she could think of was a hymn she used to sing to her little girls: *Allein, und doch nicht ganz allein...Bin ich in meiner Einsamkeit...*

Fighting despair, Magdalena Hartman began to sing the old German melody. The hymn wafted through the crowd of former captives and caught the ear of one tall girl. Slowly, she took a step, and then another, toward Magdalena. The mother's heart pounded as the girl ventured forward and nervously began to sing in a clear but trembling voice....*Allein, und doch nicht ganz....*

Magdalena was overtaken with emotion. The girl wept as she stared in the eyes of her mother for the first time in nearly ten years. Miraculously, Regina Hartman had been reunited with what was left of her family.

•

# THE LAST DUEL IN PENNSYLVANIA

The final time two feuding individuals were supposed to have been able to settle their differences by drawing pistols and engaging in a duel should have been 1794, when the practice was outlawed by the Commonwealth of Pennsylvania.

But, what is believed to have been the last classic duel fought in the state was fought in **Mahanoy City** on March 26, 1931.

History has not recorded what prompted mineworkers Savo Raicevich and Risto Brankovich to choose pistols as their arbiters, but it was according to their Montenegrin custom that they met on the N. 8th St. dumping grounds and exchanged some 30 rounds from behind trees and rocks in their one-on-one gunfight. Both men were wounded, but Raicevich's wounds proved fatal. Brankovich was arrested and while being held in prison, he tried to commit suicide. He was eventually acquitted.

# The Angel of the Mines

Jim Ney is convinced that an apparition that came to call in a mine near **New Philadelphia** saved his life not once–but twice.

Stories of actual ghostly sightings in the coal mines are surprisingly uncommon amongst miners. But, Jim's encounter is very much in line with unexplainable phenomena several miners have reported while they faced peril deep beneath the soil.

Jim worked in the "coal hole" as an independent, and will never forget the visions that may well have been his salvation on two occasions.

"I was shoveling by a chute to load the car,"

he recalled. "I was kneeling down, shoveling, when I saw a big, white–I don't know what it was–a ghost, smoke? Whatever it was, it made me jump up. And, when I jumped, that whole thing pushed down. I got covered up to my neck. But, I wasn't crushed.

"The second time, I was up on a four-foot vein and I was working the east side while my brother was working the west side, right off the slope. It happened again!"

That second time, Jim was kneeling when he was distracted by a white figure that took shape before his startled eyes.

Suddenly, rocks began to fall from the walls and roof of the vein and he was trapped. Had he not moved swiftly from his position when he saw the white figure, he may have been crushed. As it was, his brother was able to relieve the pressure of the stones and jack the rock from atop him. He suffered some bruises, but no broken bones or serious injuries.

Was he saved by the apparitions?

"Oh, I know I was," he said with an air of confidence and relief. "I definitely believe in them. I mean, if it would have been just that one time, but that second time convinced me."

Stories of "Guardian Angels" in shafts and pits circulate through any mining culture. While that is the moniker given to the apparitions by some miners, others simply cannot attribute their presence to anything necessarily "angelic" and recall them only as "apparitions."

Such an incident created international news in 1963 when three miners were trapped more than 300 feet underground when the Fellin Coal Co. mine near **Sheppton** collapsed. Two men lived to tell the stories. One man's body was never found.

August 13, 1963 began as any other working day for Dave Fellin, Henry Throne, and Louis Bova. By eight in the morning, the three had already filled up a buggy at the very bottom of the shaft.

Louis Bova gave the signal, the buggy was sent to the top and emptied. As it was coming back down, Henry Throne said, "that's when the big rumble started and all hell broke loose."

Timbers caved in, stones and coal and wood tumbled all around them. Throne and Fellin were on one side of the rubble and Bova was trapped on the other. The work lights broke immediately, and the only light was that from the fast-fading helmet lamps. Then, they too burned out and the three men were in total darkness.

The rumbling continued for more than an hour and sporadically after that. Henry Throne called out for Louis Bova, but there was no response. Incredible tales of survival were told by Throne and Fellin. They ate bark from the timber and sucked rancid water from it. For 14 horrendous days the men were sealed in a cramped mine tunnel the length of a football field underground. For more than five of those days, they had no light whatsoever.

During that time, as Throne later reported to the press, he and David Fellin experienced a macabre series of sightings.

"I'd sleep, I'd wake up, and I'd see all kinds

*Louis Bova's grave at the site of the 1963 mine collapse near Sheppton.*

of light and the actual figures of people," Throne told the *Pottsville Republican*. "The lights and the figures always were in front of us but the more we crawled toward them the further away they got. For example, I saw this man, or the dark shape of a man with a light on his helmet. I yelled 'Show me some light over here!' Davey saw him too, but the shape of the man got smaller and smaller as we crawled toward him and then he was gone altogether."

The survivors also told reporters they had a vision of Pope John XXIII, who had died two months before the mine collapse.

What's more, they said they saw doors that beckoned to be open but vanished as they approached them.

The most poignant contact was when, on about the sixth day of their entrapment, both men claim that they heard Louis Bova yell, "Davey, Hank? Where are you? This is Louis, I have a light!"

That was the last they, or anyone, ever heard from Louis Bova.

The 42-year old miner's body was never recovered. On August 26, Throne and Fellin were rescued after a reamer plunged into the deep tunnel and they were carried to the top in harnesses.

Were what Throne reported only illusions or delusions? "They told me they were hallucinations," Throne said, "but the crazy thing is that Davey would see the same things I did."

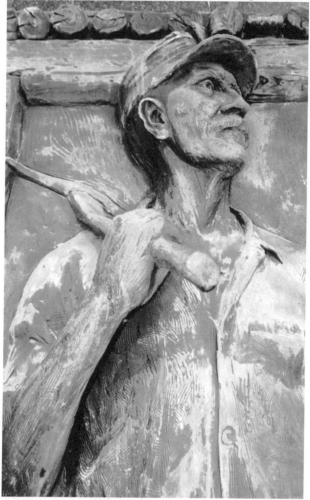

*Detail from the Miners' Memorial, Shenandoah.*

## Are Spirits Brewing at the Kaier Mansion?

Does the ghost of "Champagne Charlie" Kaier walk within the walls of his former home in the heart of **Mahanoy City**? Do the spirits of spinster sisters who once resided there still glide over its floorboards?

Jane Goodman simply offers a coy grin and a shrug when those questions are asked.

Jane has fashioned a fashionable bed & breakfast inn out of the handsome home that has seen its share of intrigue over the years.

"It was always rumored that when people would pass here they would tremble because it was believed to be haunted," Jane said.

The Schuylkill County native and professional real estate agent purchased the Kaier Mansion in 1991 and after she examined its lavish rooms, hand-carved woodwork, stained glass windows, and spectacular appointments she envisioned transforming it into a B&B. The following year, the transformation was complete.

The circa 1870 Victorian structure was home to generations of the Kaier family, namesakes of the brewery that once was among Mahanoy City's leading employers and important businesses. It was built by Charles D. and Margaret Kaier, founders of the brewery.

As those generations of Kaiers lived and died in what they called "The Residence," many a tale emerged from within its walls.

According to the family history, one teenage

daughter, Marie, caused considerable scandal when she eloped with a Shenandoah blacksmith's son and prompted her mother to send a Pinkerton detective to track her down. Marie was brought back, but was soon disinherited after refusing to leave her new husband.

The early 20th century brought much squabbling, court battles over wills, and estrangements as the brewery boomed and the Kaier family structure went bust.

With millions of dollars hanging in the balance, the family fortune was eventually bestowed by the courts to Mame Kaier Fahler and Charles F. Kaier, two of the founder's six children.

Charles F. Kaier was reputedly free and easy with his share of the inheritance. His extravagance and irresponsibility led him to be dubbed "Champagne Charlie."

Lurid allegations and sexual scandals plagued him and, when a Philadelphia newspaper linked his name to a murdered call girl, what was left of the family was so embarrassed and humiliated that it took immediate action to remove him from Mahanoy City and their lives.

"Champagne Charlie" had resided in the mansion with his sister and her husband, but his flamboyant lifestyle led Mame to petition the courts to have him removed as co-executor of the estate. Her request was granted, and Charles was removed from the will, removed from the mansion, and given a small stipend and the family's shore home in Ventnor, New Jersey.

These details may or may not be germane to the strange sensations that have been reported in the Kaier Mansion in recent years.

"Different people have heard different things," Jane Goodman said. "Items are moved around, and several guests have reported hearing things moving."

The most intriguing story about the mansion is that of the rumored murder there of a man who was caught cheating during a card game in the dining room.

In a tale worthy of Edgar Allan Poe, it is said that in the killer's haste to cover up the crime, the victim's body was entombed within the walls of the basement. Those remains, it is said, still remain.

The dining room, with its hardwood parquet floor, chestnut molding ceiling, etched-glass chandelier, and 13 lion head chairs grouped around a 12-foot hand-carved oak table is among the mansion's most opulent rooms. And, to at least one woman, it was the setting for a bit of a surprise.

Jane Goodman told of a recent guest who had been reading in the parlor on a quiet evening. She decided to retire for the night, and crossed through the dining room to return a glass to the kitchen.

Although she was not consuming spirits that evening, she claims she was confronted by a spirit who, in a soft, spooky voice, said "hello!" as she walked through the dining room.

"She was convinced there was a ghost in the dining room," Jane added.

Quite elegant, inviting, and comfortable, the Kaier Mansion can hold its own against any bed & breakfast inn anywhere. It is, as its innkeeper rightfully claims, "a masterpiece" that has seen its share of human drama play out within its walls over the years.

Perhaps those dramas continue, and await a willing audience.

*A vintage post card:*
*"Greetings from the Anthracite Coal Regions"*

# THE PEDDLER'S GRAVE

First, what you see above is not the Peddler's Grave.

It is a badly and sadly deteriorated graveyard on the Brandonville Road hill north of **Mahanoy City**. It has been mistaken by some as the Peddler's Grave, but it is a forgotten and forsaken cemetery where the dignity of the dead has been tragically trampled upon by vandals and neglect and where its eternal residents rest in pieces.

It is not far from the nearly-inaccessible grave of Jost Folhaber, who is known in local lore simply as "The Peddler."

Most folks around Mahanoy City seem to have all-but forgotten about poor Jost, know little about who he was and what happened to him, and can scantly recall exactly where his once-famous grave is situated.

There once was a time that Jost's final resting place, or at least the approximate spot where his body was discovered, was marked by a headstone and footstone, and his tale was told in the epitaph:

| JOST FOLHABER |
|---|
| NEAR THIS SPOT WAS COMMITTED THE FIRST KNOWN MURDER IN THIS SECTION FOLHABER, A TRAVELING PEDDLER, WAS AMBUSHED, CRUELLY MURDERED AND ROBBED HE AND HIS HORSE WERE LEFT TO DIE BY THE WAYSIDE HIS ASSAILANT WAS TRIED, FOUND GUILTY, AND HANGED |

Just who was Jost? How old was he when he was slain? Where was his home town? Nobody really knows.

What history has recorded is that Jost was passing through what is now Mahanoy City in August, 1797, and happened to tarry at the tavern of John Reich (or, in some accounts, Reisch).

There, he met Benjamin Bailey, who was in the area from his native Morristown, N.J.

At the tavern, Folhaber supposedly told Bailey about his exploits as a peddler, and may well have sealed his fate by bragging to Bailey of his successes.

If that happened, Bailey realized that Folhaber's sack and saddlebags may have contained a good sum of money.

As the shards of history are ground into the powder of legend, it is generally accepted that after the two men engaged in conversation and Folhaber left the tavern to continue on his way over the mountain and into Ringtown.

Unbeknownst to Folhaber, Bailey followed him, intent on robbing him somewhere on the dense, forested hillside.

It is said that when Bailey finally accosted Folhaber along the old Catawissa Trail, he shot the salesman in the back. Folhaber was wounded, but not fatally. As he writhed in pain, Bailey completed his vile crime by burying an ax in Folhaber's skull.

As the legend lapses into pure speculation, it is further said that when Bailey rummaged through Folhaber's packs, he found only three pennies, a pitiful selection of wares, and that Folhaber had boasted falsely at the tavern about his peddling prowess.

After killing Folhaber, Bailey left his body to rot. Some accounts say Folhaber's horse was also killed on the site, and its carcass, as well as the decomposed body of the peddler, was found on August 26, 1797.

Despite the wild isolation of the region at the time, word spread quickly from village to village of the robbery and murder.

Bailey made his own fatal mistake a few weeks after his dastardly deeds by trying to sell some of his ill-gotten goods near Mifflinburg, Pennsylvania. He was arrested there and returned to Schuylkill County (then Berks County) for his trial.

Despite his plea of innocence and attempts to implicate the tavernkeeper, Bailey was found guilty and sentence to hang.

Just before the noose was to snap his neck, Bailey asked for mercy and confessed. Moments later, on January 8, 1798, on the gallows of Berks County Prison in what is now City Park in Reading, Benjamin Bailey was pronounced dead.

Since the discovery of the peddler's body, tales of ghostly activity at his grave have persisted. One version is that on occasion, and definitely on the anniversary of his murder, his horse and he appear, galloping on the mountain. The wild thumping of the horse's hooves and a bloodcurdling scream echo in the night, and in a fierce and fiery flash, the ghostly horse and rider vanish.

# MAYHEM AT MAHANOY PLANE

*In 1900, a particular house described only as "occupied by a railroader named Reicheldarfer" at Mahanoy Plane drew much attention in the local press when it was reported to be haunted-very haunted.*

*"The sights the members of the family claim to have seen during their residence in the house are calculated to make the flesh of the most unsuperstitious person crawl," reported the Pottsville Republican.*

*So terrified was the family that it fled the house after several episodes that played out there.*

*Nearly every night, they said they would hear "a series of unearthly groans and wails" coming from the cellar, followed by "the sounds of ghostly footfalls slowly climbing the cellar steps and passing along the hallway."*

*The disembodied footsteps were accompanied by "clanking, as of rusty chains dragged across the floor." The sound proceeded up the stairs to the attic, where it would reach a crescendo of "demonic laughter that would freeze the blood of the bravest man."*

*The horror ended with the sound of muffled sobs and wails, the footsteps retracing themselves back into the cellar, and "a series of hair-curling sounds too horrible for description."*

# The Hex Cat

The exact location of the farm has been lost in history, but somewhere between **Orwigsburg** and **Tumbling Run** on the southern slope of **Second Mountain** there once was a farm that came to be called the "Hex Cat Farm."

By the 1940s, when the story was presented in a *Pottsville Journal* article, the farm had already been abandoned and there was little physical evidence that it ever existed. But, around the turn of the 20th century, that farm was the center of a story that was rooted in the mysterious and nefarious practice of "hexerei."

Hexerei–as in witchcraft.

Pottsville native Howell Thomas had left the mines and turned to farming sometime around 1900. His death in 1911 sparked a family controversy that boiled over with charges of wickedness and witchcraft.

Thomas had been in good health until he suffered a stroke and complications that would claim his life after five agonizing months of suffering.

Even before his body was in its grave, Thomas' daughter, Mary, claimed that her father's suffering was not natural, but was the result of a curse placed on him by another daughter.

Moreover, she charged that a series of bizarre events prior to her father's death were the work of the "hex."

Cows and horses died suddenly, crops failed–and all of the troubles on the farm and with her father, she said, started when an ominous black cat showed up on the farm.

It was a fierce, fearful feline. Truly believing that it was responsible for her father's and the farm's ailments, she attempted to kill the cat. She swore to a neighbor that as she fired at the beast, it grew in size to four or five feet tall and long. She said the cat had the power to silence pistols and reasoned that should she ever actually kill it, its spirit may do more harm in death than in life.

Mary Thomas' wild accusations became well known on the farms between the mountain and Orwigsburg at the time. It is known that she actually contacted "fortune tellers," mystics, and "healers" from as far away as California in an attempt to resolve the situation.

In her mind, the horrid resolution was the death of her father. The "hex cat" had committed the ultimate act.

The story became even more twisted when, at her father's funeral, she became hysterical and accused one of her own sisters with placing the cat–and the curse–on the father and farm.

So emotional was Mary when she leveled the charge that she fainted after screaming the allegations over her father's dead body.

As she recovered whatever was left of her senses and awoke from her fainting spell, she went one step farther by implying that her sister's vile spirit was actually embodied in the "hex cat."

It was reported that the day after the funeral, Mary and some neighbors succeeded in killing the "hex cat," and nailing it to the side of a barn.

For a time after the odd incident, curious locals would come to the farm to gawk at the cat's decaying corpse, and for several Halloweens until the story faded, children would fashion "hex cat" costumes. Some also believed the spirit of the cat remained, and would someday rise again to cast yet another curse.

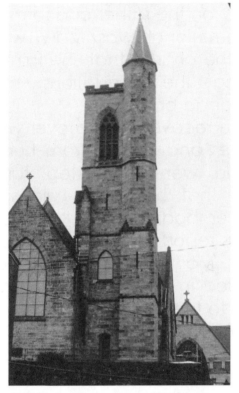

# THE GHOST OF ST. MARK'S

If any singular spirit lingers in **Jim Thorpe**, it would likely be that of Mary Packer Cummings, daughter of Asa Packer.

She was a *grand dame* in the town in which she endowed cultural, religious, civic, and social endeavors with the financial fruits of her inheritance.

In life, Mary was ever-present on the

**40**

# Coal Country Ghosts, Legends, and Lore

sidewalks of old Mauch Chunk. There are those who believe that Mary's ghost still strolls those sidewalks and pays calls occasionally on some of her most beloved institutions in present-day Jim Thorpe.

The streets of town are quiet after the shops have closed and the tourists have turned in for the night. It is then, beneath the faux-gas lamps of Broadway and on the steps and alleys that weave between the streets when Mary's ubiquitous energy may be sensed.

It may be a waft of warmth on a chilly evening or an icy burst on a warm one. Mary may manifest as a hair-raising brush upon the shoulder, a faint whisper, or the muffled crackle of crinoline that passes by.

One of Mary Packer's most venerated and visible legacies looms over the town like a Gothic bastion. It is the fortress of faith called St. Mark's Episcopal Church.

"Really though, this is Mary Packer's church."

The words are those of the Rev. Canon Kenneth S. Umbehocker, rector of St. Mark's. He cannot dismiss a variety of incidents that offer evidence that Mary's ghost has been felt, heard, and seen within the walls of the historic and handsome edifice.

The notion of a ghost inside a church is

unusual to this writer and could be unsettling to some readers. But, to Rev. Umbehocker, it is well within the perimeters of possibility.

"It's not unheard of that ghosts wander around churches," he said. "As long as it's a friendly ghost, that's fine."

What's more, he is not alone in his conviction that something out of the ordinary is going on inside the storied sanctuary.

Mary's ghost seems to have the run of the church. But, certain spots seem more, shall we say, "enchanted," than others.

An intriguing but essential interior architectural feature of St. Mark's is its elevator. There are few like it anywhere, and it is one of the oldest operating Otis-built lifts in the country.

The elevator was built at Mary's behest to replace what was a 40-step walkup entrance to the church. As it operates between the sanctuary and the street level, it was built to accommodate funerals by being sized to hold a coffin and six pallbearers.

"The elevator has a tendency to wander places on its own," Rev. Umbehocker said. And, he does not deny that Mary's energies may "operate" the errant equipment.

"She died in 1912," he continued, "and the elevator was put in by her. Sadly, she got one ride in it, and that was in her casket. She died just as it was being installed"

"We think that Mary regularly checks up on

*The elevator at St. Mark's church.*

her properties, here and elsewhere," Rev. Umbehocker continued. "Unexplained things happen around here all the time, and we attribute them either to Mary or her father, but it is probably Mary.

"We find things up in the Great Hall that nobody would admit to. Lights are left on or turned off, and nobody would be around to do so. The organ was put in by her, and we think that she has something to do with noises that occur in the organ chamber occasionally."

Rev. Umbehocker added that a former choir director actually reported seeing a shadowy figure cross through the sanctuary.

Not long ago, certain members of the church chorale swear they saw the strange figure of a woman lurking in the shadows inside the church. Each person who said they saw the apparition described her as wearing a long black dress, a black shawl, and had her hair pulled up in a tight bun.

Later, when the individuals happened upon a portrait of Mary Packer Cummings, each of them said, unequivocally, that the spirit they had seen in the sanctuary was that very same woman.

Still another individual, a church member who wishes to remain anonymous, reluctantly admitted he may have crossed paths with Mary.

"I was helping others do some work in the Great Hall," he said, "and I absolutely saw the figure of a woman, dressed in an old-fashioned gown or something, drift right past me. It happened in a flash, and although I really don't believe in ghosts, I know what I saw, and I suppose it was Mary. I'll never forget it."

# REAL FOLKS, REAL FEAR

The best ghost stories come from real people and their real-life experiences. Those stories, in turn, come from letters, telephone calls, and emails. Those tales are also savored best when presented in the writers' or callers' own words.

What follows is an account from a woman who detailed a series of untoward events that played out in her home and, especially in that one sanctuary all of us hope will never be invaded by invisible forces, the bedroom.

The correspondent's name and exact location of the incidents will not be disclosed, by request.

"My parents moved into an old stone house just outside **Deer Lake** in 1968," she said. "The house was built in 1812.

"Upon moving in, we began remodeling the house and then began experiencing strange activities.

"My father saw a spirit twice. Once, an old lady was standing near the edge of his bed and the other time he saw her standing at the doorway to his bedroom.

"We have heard footsteps in the middle of the night.

"My bedroom door used to fly open violently

**45**

and slam against my desk behind it. The latch to my door was even broken one time when that happened.

"I was sitting in my bed reading one night (so I know I was awake) and I felt my mattress go down like someone sat on my bed and then stood back up again.

"I was home alone one day sitting in the kitchen about noontime when it sounded like someone was dragging something heavy across the floor of my sister's bedroom above me. It sounded as if it might have been a trunk.

"My parents were away one weekend, and my girlfriend and I were meeting back at my parents' house with our dates. My girlfriend and her date arrived first and went into the kitchen to wait. While they were waiting, they heard voices talking."

The young woman who sent the letter said that after the initial flurry of activity (which followed the renovation of the house and possibly the disturbance of the energies within), things calmed down. But, more recently, a chance encounter with a psychic may have revealed more about who might have been behind the strange occurrences in the Deer Lake house.

"My cousin was visiting from Ohio," the letter continued, "and asked my mother if she could use the phone to call a friend in Ohio. While she was talking to her friend, who was a psychic, her friend started describing my mother's house very accurately.

"She also told my cousin that there were two presences that dwelled in the house.

"One was an older man named George, who had died from a fever and his favorite room was my bedroom.

"The other presence was a younger man she believed was a Native American. His name, she thought, was 'Beau.' He told her he died from a gunshot wound, and he liked to linger in the basement."

Although the guarantee of anonymity for the writer may place the level of credibility a bit lower for the reader, you must trust that the individual who wrote the previous account was very real, as were the experiences she detailed in that old home near Deer Lake.

•

Another woman who asked that her name not be published, offered another personal story that also reinforces the reality that some people can actually become "attached" to the entities that cohabit their spaces.

In this case, the story unfolds in **Port Carbon**, where a domineering and dominating ghost the homeowner calls "Mary" has caused a bit of consternation over the years.

"A lot of the kids say they have seen her," the woman noted. During crowded, rowdy sleepovers or on quiet nights at home, "Mary's" spirit has been seen and felt. And, the homeowner joked that her generally unseen companion is actually helpful at times. "She just makes sure the cupboards are closed, or the refrigerator door is closed, things like that."

The teller of the story is firmly convinced that the ghost in her house is not a figment of anyone's whimsy or imagination.

"Oh, no," she said, "we might kid around about her, but she's very real. In fact, I saw her a few times. Or, at least, I saw what I believe was her. She's, how do I describe it, *filmy*. She doesn't say anything. But, she definitely goes through the house and closes doors and moves things. She never does any harm to anyone or anything."

The woman's youngest daughter seems most sensitive to the energies that swirl in her home. She, and other family members are quite comfortable with the idea that they share their home with a ghost.

"I believe she's there," the woman said of Mary, "and, quite honestly, if her spirit ever left our house, I'd miss her!"

# Madeline...
## and the Ghosts of
## The Inn at Jim Thorpe

*Room 211, The Inn at Jim Thorpe*

"It was sometime in the late 1800s when a man and woman made reservations here–they were cheating on their spouses–but they got their wires crossed. One booked room 211, and the other checked into room 311. They never found each other. So, I was told, to this day they are still here, looking for one other."

The story was told by David Drury, owner of

the historic, charming and bustling centerpiece of downtown **Jim Thorpe**, the Inn at Jim Thorpe. While he related that story with a certain air of cynicism, he could not dismiss a continuing series of events that has virtually every staff member at the inn convinced there are spirits that walk among them.

Drury's account of the star-crossed lovers stems from the speculations of a Lehigh Valley psychic who "saw" the chain of events in a reading of the inn a few years ago. The psychic's revelations included the belief that the young woman was so distressed about the doomed rendezvous that she took her own life in her room.

That room, all at the inn are convinced, was Room 211.

While there is no indication what the woman's name was, an inn employee arbitrarily called the spirit "Madeline" after it tormented her.

Thus, most of the spectral activities at the inn have since been blamed–rightly or wrongly–on Madeline.

Does David Drury buy into the findings of the psychic? "Well," he said, "it was pretty bizarre, because she described over the phone what room it was occurring in. She didn't give the room number, but she said you go to the top of the stairs, make a left turn, and it's the first door on the right. That, of course, is Room 211. Now, I had never talked to her before, and she said she had never been here. I thought, how could she possibly know all that."

There is a moderate, but constant level of intensity to the haunting of The Inn at Jim Thorpe. Several employees and guests, some who had never heard the story of Madeline, have reported unnerving experiences.

"There was a couple that woke up in the morning in Room 211," Drury continued, "and found that their bathroom was in total disarray. Everything was thrown all over the place. Towels were stuffed in the toilet bowl. They knew nobody else here, and there was nobody here who could have played a practical joke on them. Their door was locked, and nobody could ever explain it."

Although he tries his best to distance himself from the situation, Drury admits he has had his own brushes with the spirit energies that seem to most certainly dwell there and, all too often, intermingle and interfere with more conventional energies.

On numerous occasions, televisions in rooms at the inn have turned themselves on or off with no one around them.

Once, David Drury and a local decorator were on the third floor hanging pictures in rooms and the hallway. Drury had ascertained at the front desk that the rooms on that floor were not occupied. Still, as the two men made their way down the hall, they distinctly heard a television blaring from one of the rooms. They approached the room, certain no one was inside. Still, they knocked on the door, and as they knocked, there was a *click* from within and sound of the TV ceased. Drury checked again, and the room was indeed empty–of any living guests.

That room was number 310, and along with rooms 211 and 311, it is where many incidents have plagued many employees. One member of the housekeeping staff, Linda Green, said she was making the bed in room 310 when, as she told writer Marigrace Heyer of the *Times News*, "I heard a woman laugh. It sounded like she was right behind me and she was trying to sound like a little girl."

Janet Marsolick, a longtime employee and manager of the inn, has her own very profound story to tell about Room 211 and the corridor that leads to it.

"We had a power outage," she remembered, "and I was going down the hall giving out flashlights.

"I was walking, just swinging my flashlight when I saw her. I could see her hair, and she had a beautiful dress, yellow with little flowers all over it. I couldn't see any arms or anything. But, she just disappeared through the door...of Room 211."

Still another worker at the inn recalled two incidents that miffed guests in Room 211. In her *Times News* article about the inn's ghosts, Marigrace Heyer spoke with desk clerk Carolyn Kelly, who received the report of the towels in the toilet incident.

"Kelly said another guest in 211 complained that he kept getting wakeup calls at 11 o'clock every night," Heyer reported. "A check with the wakeup service showed no one had ever called that room.

"It's not unusual any more, says Kelly, to hear stories from guests about finding their shoes or bedroom slippers on the opposite side of the room from where they placed them the preceding night."

Another phenomenon that has baffled many workers at the inn was recalled by innkeeper David Drury.

"The person who works overnight told me a few times that the ceiling fans in the restaurant would go on–they'd just start spinning around on their own and then they'd just shut off.

"I did witness it one time when I came in early. I couldn't explain it because the kitchen is closed, locked, padlocked–nobody can get in there. And, in order to control the fans, you must be in the kitchen. I know for a fact there was no one in the kitchen at that time. It was pretty bizarre."

Janet Marsolick has also witnessed the self-spinning ceiling fans on several occasions. They only served to bolster her beliefs that the Inn at Jim Thorpe is haunted by a harmless, but at times quite mischievous ghost.

"I never believed in ghosts, never, never," Janet shrugged. "That is, not until things started going on here. Now, I guess I'm convinced."

The inn takes its haunting seriously. It has staged "Ghost Hunters Weekends," when it hosts members of the Philadelphia Ghost Hunters Alliance who present discussions of ghosts in general and investigations of the inn's ethereal residents.

In previous investigations at the inn, the PGHA team detected significant levels of activity at several locations throughout the building.

While some of that activity was recorded in the "usual suspects" of Rooms 211, 310, and 311, at least two other rooms and the unoccupied fourth floor of the building also yielded enough psychic and electronic anomalies to lead the researchers to conclude that there is spirit energy there, and it warrants further and closer examination.

# SPIRITS OF SUMMIT HILL

It could be said that the **Summit Hill** Historical Society owes a debt of gratitude to the ghosts of the hilltop Carbon County town.

"When we formed the historical society," said David Wargo, "one of the first fundraising projects I suggested was a ghost tour." That, he added, was well before walking tours of haunted places popped up in town after town across Coal Country and beyond.

Wargo is a magician, Summit Hill borough councilman, officer and founding member of the historical society, and the author of "Mysteries on the Mountain: A Collection of Summit Hill Folklore." That was his only published title at the time this book was being written, but he had plans to research and write other companion books about the lore of other towns in the Panther Valley.

Wargo and fellow historian Jerry Matika were interviewed in the historical society's museum on Ludlow Street, where they took turns speaking of the interviews and investigations they and others have conducted.

As the "Panther Valley Paranormal Society," the group joined the ranks of those who have plunged into ghostly research armed with digital recorders, cameras, temperature and motion detectors...and good, old-fashioned psychic talents.

"We started doing research on ghost stories in Summit Hill," Wargo said, "because my theory was that in a town like this where life was hard for a couple hundred years, ghost would appear where there have been problems, and where there were premature deaths. So, there had to be ghost stories here."

# Coal Country Ghosts, Legends, and Lore

Summit Hill lays claim as the birthplace of the Industrial Revolution as it was the source of some of the first coal that reached markets in Philadelphia in the early 19th century. In its streets once lurked members of the Molly Maguires, and in an unmarked grave behind one of the town's churches lies the body of Alexander Campbell, a "Molly" who may or may not have left an eternal, indelible hand print at the old Carbon County Jail–a story detailed elsewhere in this volume.

As Wargo and others fanned out to gather ghost stories in Summit Hill, they faced some resistance.

"Ghosts were frowned upon up here," he lamented "Even though people had their experiences, they hesitated talking about them. But, since we started collecting the stories, people realized we were treating them and their stories with respect, and more and more people came forward."

What sparked Wargo's interest in the supernatural was what is arguably the most famous ghost of Summit Hill, the "Lady in White" at one of the eight cemeteries at the end of town.

"There is so much to that story," Wargo continued, "so many people who have corroborated the story over the years, that I was fascinated by it. So, we decided to do some empirical research to better document the cemetery and what goes on there."

Wargo admitted that the story has mutated over the years.

"The most ambitious version of the Lady in White story," he noted, "is that a woman appears in the cemetery at the time of the full moon and wanders through and then out of the cemetery and heads toward the town—but never quite makes it to town. She just vanishes somewhere along the way.

"The more likely story, and the one that I've heard from people who say they've experienced it, is that she appears in the cemetery late at night and just breezes through, almost as if she's inspecting the cemetery."

Jerry Matika has also heard the stories.

"There's another twist to it," he said. "I've heard that the woman's child was buried in the back corner of the cemetery, and she appears late at night, grieving for her lost child."

A portion of the old switchback railroad, which connected Summit Hill with Mauch Chunk (Jim Thorpe) runs adjacent to the cemetery, and one of the historical society's first projects was an attempt to restore the trail, which had been overgrown and strewn with litter. As that project was underway, volunteers constantly reported eerie sensations, cold spots, and sensations that someone was peering over their shoulders.

"I know what they felt," Wargo said. "It's a strange, strange feeling there."

Using established and accepted paranormal investigation techniques, Wargo and others were taking photographs of the cemetery. "During that expedition," Wargo said, "I felt an overwhelming sense of suffocation there. What's more, one of the men who was with me, who speaks Polish, heard a voice that told us to 'go' in Polish. So, we went!"

Matika has also had some experiences in the old graveyard. "In fact," he said, "when I first started looking into all of this, I went up there and just wandered around snapping photographs. I had my digital voice recorder, too.

"Nothing came up on the photographs, but when I listened to the recording, I heard my footsteps in the leaves, and then after I stopped, I could hear soft footsteps that seemed to be following me."

Stories of ghostly encounters in the cemeteries of Summit Hill are not a recent phenomenon.

"I spoke to guys who used to play football up there on the hill before the cemeteries were expanded," Wargo said. "Back then, it was just a field and they used to play ball there. I talked to several older men who said they definitely remember seeing a mysterious woman in a white dress or white nightgown wandering up there around dusk."

This happened long before there were any notions of ghosts there. "They just thought it was a woman who lived up there and was confused." The men at that time rationalized and wrote-off her mysterious appearance as odd, but probably explainable.

Police officers, and professional people have told David and Jerry of their sightings of the Lady in White. "She has been seen all over the area," Matika said, "especially at the intersection around Route 902 and Lentz Trail.

"One day, in a light fog, a man came into the 'Switchback' (a convenience store on Route 902 just south of town) and was scared to death. He told the clerks that a woman came out of nowhere, crossed the road in front of him, and he knew he had hit her with his car. He couldn't stop...he had to have hit her. But, he told them, instead of an impact with her body, his car passed right through her!"

That story was later confirmed by a clerk at the convenience store who recalled the event quite clearly. She said the man who came into the store was visibly shaken, and was convinced that he had hit a woman with his car. Strangely, he seemed to calm down and even be amused when the store employees told him he had probably encountered the Lady in White.

Wargo smiled as he related yet another incident that involved Summit Hill's rambling wraith and an individual he chose not to identify.

"Let's just say that I can guarantee you that there is a prominent person whose credibility would be unquestioned who encountered the Lady in White along the Lentz Trail. He saw her when he was going to work at about four o'clock one morning. Basically, he described her as standing on the side of the road, dressed in a cross between a nightgown and a shroud–he really wasn't sure–and she was trying to wave him down. From what he told me, when he drove past her he tried to think of how he could help her without stopping. He figured he'd get to work, which was nearby, and call for help for her. But as he watched her, she just disappeared!"

As Wargo detailed in his book, there are several places in and near Summit Hill where ghosts wander.

One is an old road that leads from Lansford to Summit Hill. The locals called it the "Indian Steps."

"There used to be a dance hall there, and supposedly, there were several incidents in the early 1900s when people would be harassed by shadows and spirits as they came through the woods from the town and back. I was told that an Episcopal priest was actually asked to bless the area. They say the place was once the site of muggings of several miners who were coming home with the pay. Back then, they were paid in gold, and the story goes that some miners were waylaid, and maybe even murdered there. It would be their ghosts that remain."

Jerry Matika has found his hometown to be a fertile source of paranormal phenomena. His own interests in the topic are deeply rooted.

"I grew up in a house that my parents told me somebody had died in," he said. "And, we'd see shadows every time we'd turn around. My parents bought the house in the 1960s, and learned that an old man had lived there–they called him a miser. He was found dead there one morning, wrapped in a carpet. Ever since then, I heard the stories of seeing shadows in the house, and things like that."

When he and others formed the local paranormal investigation group, he found his true mission in life.

"At every turn, I look for something of the paranormal or supernatural," he said. "They're out there. They're not out to hurt you, but they *are* out there."

And for Dave Wargo, his interest in ghost could be considered a natural extension of being a magician by trade.

As a youth, he discounted many ghost stories he heard, but as his sensitivity sharpened, he grew to better understand what dwells on the other side–and inside his home town.

## THE GHOSTLY HEAD

While "headless ghosts" are often encountered in legends and folklore, there is an ancient tale of "The head of a trunkless man" that haunted Long Swamp in
**West Brunswick Township,**
Schuylkill County. It was said that the disembodied head could be heard speaking, pleading for anyone who passed by to find its body, unite it with the corpse, and give it a proper burial.

*Mauch Chunk (now Jim Thorpe), ca. 1930*

# The Ghost Cat of the Emporium

Barrett Ravenhurst is somewhat of an enigma in **Jim Thorpe**. He has a doctorate in comparative religions, and he is a Wiccan, a practitioner of the religion more commonly known as "witchcraft."

A successful professional magician for more than three decades, Ravenhurst settled into a comfortable life as a merchant in Jim Thorpe, where he owns and operates a Wiccan/New Age/Metaphysical shop aptly named "The Emporium of Curious Goods."

He is likely the only Wiccan to ever chair a town's Olde Time Christmas celebration on behalf of the Chamber of Commerce. But, Barrett's that kind of man–an enigma.

When any would-be ghost hunter comes to Jim Thorpe, their first stop would likely be Barrett's funky and freaky shop. And while it seems as if the place should be infested with spirits, it harbors only one–a ghostly cat.

"It's a big, gray cat," Barrett said. "Kids often sense it, but we've had several adults report its presence."

It should be noted that Barrett has cats–live cats–in his shop, but the phantom feline that is sensed and sometimes seen by the more sensitive types who enter his aromatic emporium is not one of them.

"A couple of times," he noted, "particularly in the hallway upstairs, as I was shaving and the bathroom door would be open, I would see a cat walk by."

Barrett would stop shaving and try to take a better, longer look at the creature.

Just as he would fix a gaze on it, it would vanish.

He was certain he had seen a cat. But, it was no alley or house-variety cat.

"Well, this is difficult to describe," he continued. "But, the strange thing is that the cat

I would see upstairs was walking upright, like a heraldic lion figure."

Barrett further described the beast as being rather large for a cat, perhaps 18 inches long.

Every once in a while, a customer comments to Barrett about the large, strange cat they have seen in the shop, especially in the rear area.

"The back of the store was once a small theater," he said. "There was a curtain that divided it from the rest of the shop. The bottom of that curtain was often seen ruffled and maybe flipping up and back down again, as if a cat was walking under it. But, none of my cats was back there. It was very, how shall I say, curious!"

*Is this a picture of ghostly activity
at the Lehighton Legion hall?*

# Lehighton's
# Haunted Legion Hall

They call their spirit "Jim" at the American Legion No. 314 on Bridge Street in **Lehighton**. and, they believe it is the presence of the man who was a guiding spirit of the founding of the post.

"Jim" was James W. Blakslee (1870-1926), an assistant Postmaster General during the administration of President Woodrow Wilson and the man who conveyed the title of his home to the American Legion.

Nearly everyone who spends any time at the Legion Hall is convinced that Jim's energy has made an eternal imprint there.

"He's here," said Becky Johnson, "there's no doubt about that. Now, I've never seen him, but others say they have."

Becky is the steward at the club. She, as well as office workers, bartenders, and other workers have their stories to tell.

One morning when one of the women office workers there came in to open the club, she saw a man sitting at one of the tables. He was described as, literally and figuratively, a "little old man."

The employee was taken aback. She figured he was an unfortunate chap who was locked into the building after it had closed the previous night and as she looked at him she uttered, "Oh, my God! What are you doing here??"

She scarcely finished the question when the man simply vanished.

Later, she compared the face she had seen to the face of a man on a portrait that hangs at the entrance to the club. It was the face of James Blakslee.

Bartender Joanne Graver recalled other strange happenings.

"We have candles that are lit when we're sure nobody lit them. And, the ghost–Jim–seems to hate eagles for some reason. We had a ceramic figure of an eagle, and when nobody was near it, it fell over and shattered. Pictures of eagles fall of the walls. We blame it on the ghost."

Another barkeep, Dick Fink, confirmed the candle and lighting quirks, and even said he has seen dim figures seeming to lurk behind the bar on occasion.

Once, a group of employees toyed with a Ouija Board and asked if "Jim" were there, and content. "It went right to 'yes,'" quipped Joanne Graver.

Like the old jail up the road in Jim Thorpe with its indelible hand print of a condemned criminal, the Legion Hall in Lehighton has its own permanent print.

"It's a real noticeable hand print," Johnson said. "And, it's on a metal cooler door. We tried to wipe it off, but no way was that hand print coming off!"

Johnson and others at the Legion are uncertain as to the origin of the print, but they are adamant that cleaning, scrubbing, and even scraping does nothing. The hand print may seem to vanish for a while, but it always returns despite efforts to eradicate it.

What further "spooked" those at the Legion Hall was he experience of Derrick Ruben, who was downstairs, repairing some kitchen equipment, in close proximity to the hand print.

As he finished the job, he heard a man's voice that seemed to echo from within the room. It said "Thank you." Ruben thought someone was playing a joke on him until he realized there was absolutely, positively, no man, and no one at all, anywhere nearby. All the way up the stairs to the main room, the hair stood up on his neck.

And, he was a total nonbeliever in ghosts....with the accent on *was*.

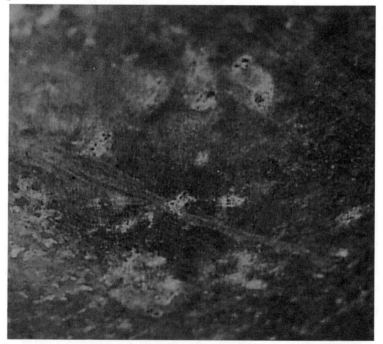

*The hand print at the Lehighton Legion Hall.*

*Albert Yashinsky, confessed killer of...*

# THE RINGTOWN WITCH

Deep in the Ringtown Valley in the darkness of the night in the dead of the winter of 1934, a gunshot rang out and became a clarion call that exposed the world not only to a heinous crime but to the tragic consequences of the deranged mind of a man who was raised in a society rife with secrets and superstitions.

Headlines would scream and stories would shout about something that folks in Coal Country would only whisper about until that fatal night on a dirt road near the Shenandoah Fish and Game Club.

"The valley, one of the most beautiful spots in eastern Pennsylvania by daylight, was, in the gloom of night a ghostly, eerie place, silent, deserted." With those words, the author of a story in *True Detective* (a magazine equivalent to today's tabloid newspapers) set the mood for what it–and newspapers in the region and nation–called the "Hex Murder."

The writer related the story of the murder of Susan Mummey, who was better known to many Schuylkill Countians as "Old Suss" or "The Ringtown Witch."

At age 67, Old Suss had established a reputation as "a creature feared and shunned by a superstitious community," according to the article. She was called a "witch" and was capable of casting spells and "hexes." Yet, some sought her for her alleged healing powers. Be it for curses or cures, Old Suss was a well-known figure in the valley and beyond.

She was a widow who lived in her simple house with an adopted daughter, Tavilla, and a boarder named Jacob Rice. Her husband, Henry, had been killed in an explosion at a powder mill in Ferndale in 1914. His body was never found.

Throughout the 20 years of her widowhood, Susan Mummey left a trail of allegations and accusations as to her ability to "pow-wow" and engage the black arts in what the old Pennsylvania Germans called "hexerei."

One of those who hated "Old Suss" the most was a 24 year old Shenandoah man named Albert Yashinsky. For reasons trapped within the vault of his mind, Yashinsky believed that the old woman had a personal vendetta against him and had placed a hex on him when his family lived near her in the mid-1920s.

He told folks that the witch had burdened him with a gigantic black cat with green eyes that would torment him every night. He claimed he would feel bony hands on his shoulders and pinpricks on his flesh, and Old Suss was to blame.

Yashinsky consulted other "pow-wowers" and medical doctors, but none could ease his anguish.

Complicating that anguish were the voices he

would hear, calling to him. Sometime in the winter of 1934, one of those voices told him to seek out and slay the witch. He made it his mission to do so and relieve himself of the demons he was certain Old Suss had cast upon him.

The night was cold and quiet in Ringtown Valley on March 17, 1934. Susan Mummey was preparing to tend to the sore feet of her boarder, Jacob Rice. Lanterns lit her parlor and, as the magazine article noted, "Old Suss moved about the room, her angular figure making grotesque shadows upon the walls, her thin lips muttering unintelligible sounds."

Unbeknownst to all in the old farmhouse, a car was coasting down the lane. The driver was the bedeviled Albert Yashinsky. Propped against the passenger's seat was a shotgun loaded with powerful "pumpkin shells."

Yashinsky lurked for only moments in a light drizzle that fell outside the Mummey house. He lifted his rifle. In his sights, silhouetted by the glow of a lamp, was Old Suss. He took dead aim. The voices swirled in his brain, and slowly and steadily his trigger finger squeezed one shot. The sound exploded and echoed in the valley. The bullet, designed to fell large game, crashed through the window and then into the heart of the witch.

Tavilla and Jacob doused the lamps and dropped to the floor. They huddled together in fear as another shot, that one more distant, was fired. Then, silence.

"As their eyes grew accustomed to the darkness," the magazine writer said, "they saw the crumpled figure of 'Old Suss,' and it was grotesque in the gloom."

It wasn't until the light of morning that Tavilla and Jacob crawled from the corner in which they cowered, not far from the lifeless corpse of the Ringtown Witch.

They hastened to a farmhouse down the road and called for the farmer to summon the police.

When investigators arrived at the Mummey house, they found the old woman in a pool of blood, her chest ripped apart by the impact of the bullet.

State and local police mounted a manhunt to find the killer of Susan Mummey. With the help of observant neighbors who had spotted a suspicious car abandoned not far from Mummey's house, Albert Yashinsky was captured, questioned, and ultimately convicted of the murder.

Damning testimony by Yashinsky's neighbors and friends revealed to police that he had talked about his hatred of Old Suss and his certainty that she had hexed him.

Ultimately, Yashinsky confessed and revealed all sordid details of the crime, and his reasons for committing it.

Incredibly, he spoke with unabashed joy about how after he was sure the witch woman was dead, he felt the evil spirits draining from his body. He sang, he smiled, he threw the gun into the woods and joined friends at a local dance hall.

He laughed when interrogators told him that his actions might send him to the electric chair. He told them he feared nothing any longer. "No matter what happens," he told Police Chief Lewis Buono of Pottsville, "nothing could be worse than what I lived through. For seven years I was a man in hell. Today, I am happy, free. I am not afraid of the future. Nothing can hurt me now."

Yashinsky was judged to be insane and was committed to the Farview Insane Asylum.

# GHOSTS OF THE BRUNO SCHOOL

Say the word "massacre" in Schuylkill and Carbon counties and the most likely word-association response will be "Indian" or "Molly Maguires."

Say the word "massacre" in **Kelayres**, and you've said it all. While it has faded in the memories of many over the decades, and while it remains a bloody blotch on the town's history, the "Kelayres Massacre" has left an indelible mark in many ways, including, some say, in a ghostly way.

77

# Coal Country Ghosts, Legends, and Lore

Near the turn of the twentieth century, the Joseph J. Bruno family gained an unbelievable foothold on virtually every phase of life in Kelayres and surrounding Kline Township. Historical documents list family members as school directors, a county detective, justice of the peace, tax collector, Coal and Iron Police officer, beer distributor, bus driver, teacher, bank vice-president, bank teller, truant officer, inspector of weights and measures, postmaster, contractor, and prominent members of the Republican party.

Did I forget to mention bootleggers? Slot machine racketeering? And philanthropy?

The Brunos were at once respected by many, feared by some, and loathed by others in the community.

So influential were family members on the highest level of the operation of schools in the area that they actually built a school that was named the "Bruno School" and staffed it with virtually hand-picked teachers, administrators, and support employees.

The Bruno family's grip on Kelayres came to a tragic, crashing end on the night of November 5, 1934, the eve of a crucial election.

Michael Petresky, a former Lehigh Valley Railroad gandy dancer who worked his way up the union ranks over the years, was 19 at the time. He said he can remember that night as if it were yesterday.

The town's Democrats had been mobilized with the intent of toppling the Bruno family's dominance. Around nine o'clock on the night before the election, they gathered on the streets of Kelayres on their way to a meeting at a supporter's home. As the group marched, it gathered strength in numbers and in fortitude. Many of them shouted "Down With the Brunos." as they approached Fourth and Centre streets.

Petresky was coming home from choir practice that night, but was drawn into the scene when the horrid cacophony of screams and gunshots erupted and turned what was a peaceful demonstration into a bloodbath.

As the throng approached Joe Bruno's house on the corner, and his son James' house next door, they no doubt taunted the family. But, they could never have expected to face what happened there that night.

At once, a hail of gunfire sprayed from the lawns, the windows, and from behind the bushes of the Bruno houses. Marchers scattered or took cover as best they could as the firing continued. Pandemonium reigned in Kelayres that night.

Michael Petresky couldn't believe his eyes. He saw the flashes of the gunshots, heard the screams, and actually thought at first that the bullets were blanks, or warning shots. Then, he saw blood. He saw men and women hit and fall.

When it was over, six people were dead, nearly two dozen were seriously wounded, and dozens more were slightly injured by ricocheting bullets or in their attempts to flee the fray.

Saladego's Drug Store, now the town's post office, and Immaculate Conception Church became refuges for many of the injured.

State police from as far away as Reading arrived in town late that night to restore order and sort out what had happened.

When police entered the Bruno houses, they found an arsenal of weapons and arrested 14 individuals who were in the houses. Several of them were convicted of murder or manslaughter.

The anti-Bruno forces had their way the next day as the Democrats scored a landslide victory in the elections.

The lock the family had on local social, political, and educational enterprises took another turn in 1937, when the name "Bruno" was removed from the front of the town's school building and replaced by "Kelayres." But, it seems, some things could not be removed.

And, several people now swear that the old school building is haunted.

# Coal Country Ghosts, Legends, and Lore

It is now the home of McAdoo Machine Company, a fabricating and machining plant owned by Gene Sobolewski. He, his son Matt, and shop employee Dennis Fenkner are among those who are convinced there are ghosts in the sprawling structure.

No one is claiming that any haunting in the school is related to the massacre, but Gene Sobolewski said, "After the massacre, people said they would hear a baby crying in the school. Usually it was at night, and it came from the basement."

As the former school was being renovated for its new life as a machine shop, many photographs were taken as the transition went on. Some yielded interesting surprises.

"On one of the pictures, against one of the walls was a figure of a guy with no head! Just a plaid shirt, standing there, as if he was posing for the picture.

But, there was nobody there. We know that. We were just taking pictures of equipment."

Another photo revealed a face by a baseboard in a hallway.

"You can actually see the outline, the eyes, the nose," Sobolewski said.

After a janitor was spooked by a the sound of a baby crying in an unfinished part of the basement, a priest was called in to bless the baby and the building.

Even after that ritual, the sounds continued. Doors opened and closed on their own. Workers report seeing fleeting glimpses of phantoms flitting about.

"At night," Matt Sobolewski said, "we'd be working and we'd hear people talking. Clanging, banging sounds would be heard, and we knew there was nobody else there."

Dennis Fenkner cited another mysterious encounter that left a handful of workers scratching their heads.

"One time," he said, "there were about six of us in one of the rooms waiting for pizza delivery. We heard a sound, saw someone come in, and watched him disappear. Let's just say it wasn't the pizza guy!"

# Annie's Miracle

Annie Sterner hadn't been able to walk, even with the aid of crutches, for eight or nine years. All of her neighbors on Mahantongo Street in Pottsville knew that for certain. Stricken at an early age with a crippling spinal disease, 25-year old Annie lived the life of an invalid, but would never give up hope of salvation from what everyone feared would be a lifelong affliction.

Every day, though, Annie prayed that her health would somehow, miraculously, be restored.

In the fall of 1883, as reported in the *Reading Daily Eagle* newspaper, Annie's prayers-and dreams-literally came true.

"A few nights ago," the story noted, "Annie retired to rest as usual. During the night she had a strange dream in which she was informed that she was cured.

"When she awoke, the impressions of her dream were still upon her mind, and she felt as if indeed she was in the realization of its truth."

Cautiously, Annie sat up on her bed. She dangled her brittle legs over the side and carefully touched her feet to the floor. She stood, and sure enough, her legs were somehow strong enough to support her.

She placed one leg ahead of the other and slowly but steadily walked across the floor of her bedroom!

In short order, Annie was able to amble several blocks into downtown Pottsville, and eventually discarded her crutches forever.

"These are the plain facts of the case," the reporter wrote. "The lady had suffered intense pain for years, and the best medical staff had failed to effect a cure. "She herself is thoroughly convinced that her restoration is a miracle."

# The
# Spirit
# on the
# Summit

The Blue Mountain Summit is positioned at the threshold of Schuylkill County at the intersection of two very busy and very different thoroughfares.

Vehicular traffic climbs the mountain until it reaches the top, where the quaint and quiet restaurant and B&B is located.

While most of the establishment's clientele arrives from that roadway, a growing number of guests trek in via the Appalachian Trail that virtually crosses its parking lot.

Even today, the Blue Mountain Summit is somewhat remote and romantic, and within its walls are many tales waiting to be told.

Innkeeper Ken Lalik recalled one of those tales. He told of guests who were staying in one of the cozy suites on the floor above the restaurant who checked out and told him their stay was restful and relaxing.

"But," Lalik said, "they did say one thing.

They told me the people in the room above them were a little loud. They said they heard clip-clop, clogging sounds on the floor above them. I fold them it was probably a squirrel or something. They said no, it was definitely footsteps.

"Then, they went outside for a walk and they looked back to their room and noticed what I knew all along-that there is no room above theirs! It sent chills down my spine." Ken had been told that there was a death many years ago in the building, "Something about a woman running up the stairs," he said. "I don't know much more about it than that."

But Mike Sechler, the live-in chef at the Blue Mountain Summit, knows that he had a very strange encounter in his room that is situated above the bar.

"It was just after I had moved in," he said, "and I was in bed. It was about three o'clock in the morning. I woke up and I thought I heard a noise. I thought it was a cat or something. Then, this thing walked in front of my bed. I looked up and wondered, 'what the heck?'"

The figure stopped, and for an awkward, unsettling moment, Mike had a better look at it. He described it as a "filmy, cloudy, female figure."

In the dark of night, he couldn't make out

much more than that. "And then," he said, "it turned and walked out the door."

And then, Mike did what any other tired young man would do in a situation such as that-he went back to sleep.

But, the encounter has puzzled him ever since. Is the Blue Mountain Summit haunted? "Oh, I don't know for sure," said Ken

"Sometimes I'll look around and might see something, but it's nothing that really stands out."

One Tamaqua area resident who worked at the restaurant several years ago and requested anonymity also heard the story of the woman who died on the stairs of the inn. "We always thought that her ghost was there," she said, "and I remember that some people said they had seen her image there. I never really believed them, but heck, you never know."

*A vintage post card view of Glen Onoko Falls*

# THE LEGEND OF GLEN ONOKO

Deep in the Lehigh Gorge in the Nesquehoning Valley there once lived the Indian brave Opachee. Not far away, but high on Locust

Mountain lived a fair maiden named Onoko.

Their story of unfulfilled passion has gone down in history as one of the most enduring legends of Carbon County.

As Opachee hunted in the forests in search of wild game to take back to his family in the valley, he met and was smitten by young Onoko.

They fell in love, but knew from the start that that love would never endure because their families did not get along. Opachee had already won the heart of Onoko, and was determined to also win the heart of her parents.

One day, he wandered the woods until he came across the biggest buck he had ever seen. With one arrow, he killed the deer and proceeded to follow a native courting custom. He would have his mother take some of the fresh venison to the parents of Onoko, and she would then prepare a succulent steak and have her mother return it to Opachee's family. The ritual would bond the families and seal the young Indians' love.

But, it was not to be. Onoko's father and mother would not be swayed. They did not want their daughter to marry the son of a rival family.

Onoko was heartbroken. She went to the cliffs of the waterfalls and hurled herself over the 60-foot cliff and onto the boulders below.

Legend has it that still today, Onoko's spirit

remains at the falls and throughout the gorge, searching forever for her lost love.

In fact, some say that every morning at 9:15, Onoko's forlorn, filmy spirit can be seen gliding across the peak of the falls.

But then again, there is another version of this legend.

Was Onoko really a dashing Delaware Indian? Was the object of his affection a maiden named Wenonah?

Was their love doomed by an angry, jealous god who drowned them in a terrible deluge as he created what is now the waterfalls and the gorge?

No matter what version–the maiden or the brave–of the legend you prefer, know that Glen Onoko is a lasting tribute to him ...or her.

*The Sarah M. McCool Room at the Angel Rose*

# Is a Whimsical Wraith an Eternal Guest at a Pottsville B&B?

Diane Karpulk has called it a "dream house." Indeed, the Angel Rose B&B at 616 W. Market Street in **Pottsville** has been featured on tours of architecturally and aesthetically important homes in Pottsville and has drawn rave reviews from guests since it opened as a bed and breakfast in 2000.

It is the quintessential Victorian charmer, a

house that would be quite at home in such places as Cape May, Charleston, or Savannah.

But, it is in Pottsville, just off Garfield Square, and its exterior appearance belies what waits within.

Passing through the front door of the Angel Rose is like passing back in time through the decades to the Victorian age. Innkeepers Bob and Diane Karpulk have created a spectacular retreat that affords all the comforts of the twenty-first century with all the charms of the nineteenth.

And, the are convinced their beloved B&B may have a guest who just won't go away.

It's nothing to fear, nothing that has ever caused concern, but it is an ethereal energy that seems to find its way into the infrastructure of the home from time to time.

Signs that the Karpulks may forever share their B&B and home with previous residents began to show themselves shortly after they moved there. "Bob smelled a perfume in the basement," Diane remembered. "It was what he described as a 'Victorian lady's' perfume, not like what I wear. It was a very heavy aroma. Another time, he picked up the pungent aroma of body odor down there."

Bob and Diane are both sensible, rational types who are not prone to jump to conclusions after one or two inexplicable incidents. But, the incidents kept coming as they settled into their new home and prospective hostelry. Television sets and other appliances would turn themselves on, and even after electricians and other tradesmen checked and double-checked all the building's systems, the electrical anomalies continued to manifest.

"We felt we were being checked out," Diane said. "It was as if someone is here, and continues to test us."

As the electrical devices–TVs, stereos, radios–seemed to have minds of their own, Bob and Diane literally pulled the plugs on the least-used equipment to ensure they would not switch on at an inopportune time.

Ironically, though, one such incident actually worked in Diane's favor.

"The strangest thing that happened to me was when we were sleeping in the front bedroom (now the Sarah M. McCool Room) and the telephone rang in the adjoining space (now the Judge Berger Room). That adjoining room was unused at the time, the shades were drawn, and it was pitch-black dark there. You couldn't see a thing in there, and the rug was rolled up, because it wasn't being used.

"But, that's where the telephone was, so when it rang, I jumped out of bed and went through the door into that room. I started to shout to Bob 'I can't see in here...,' but before I could finish the sentence, the light on a table near the door went on and I was able to go in and answer the phone without bumping into something or tripping over the rolled-up rug.

"I came back after answering the phone and I thanked Bob for turning on the light. He looked at me and told me that he didn't. He said he never got out of bed. The light went on by itself!'"

The innkeepers feel there is a guardian, a whimsical wisp that oversees the transition from private home to private home *and* B&B.

Bob does not rule out the possibility that the previous owners' spirits may still dwell there.

Once, Bob was downstairs and found a curious, unmarked cassette tape. He placed it into a player and on one side, church music played. There was no incident.

He flipped the cassette over, and the Notre Dame University "fight song" was heard. With that, one speaker, and then another, flipped from their stands.

"I don't know," Bob said, "but the previous owners were Italian-Americans, and they didn't like hearing the 'Fightin' Irish' music!

Family members and guests still detect various and sundry sensory signals that the Angel Rose may be inhabited by unseen guests.

Diane, a Minersville native and teacher there, is quite comfortable in the home and business she and Bob have put their hearts and souls into preserving and improving.

The footsteps that some visitors have heard on the main staircase and top floor, the cold spots noticed by one or two "sensitive" guests there, and the general sensation that they are never really alone does not faze her or her husband.

In fact, Diane mellowed as she remembered yet another one of those sensory signals. "I have smelled pipe smoke at various places in the house," she said. "It's a good smell. My father used to smoke a pipe," she added.

# ANTIQUES AND ANTICS IN DEER LAKE

It's a challenge for a mortal to maneuver between the thousands of antiques and collectibles that pack every room of building along Route 61 in **Deer Lake**.

But, it seems as if energies that dwell within the log, mortar, stone, and brick walls of the eighteenth-century structure have easy access to all areas.

That's the opinion not only of Judy and Sam at Judy B Antiques Collectibles, but of researchers who have uncovered a reasonable amount of evidence to convince them that the building is haunted.

One of the researchers Judy called to give the place the once-over detected a spiral shaft of energy that swept through the front basement, first floor foyer of the shop and second floor bathroom in the Boltons' upstairs living quarters.

That might frighten some people, but the Boltons are comfortable with the possibility. In fact, when he learned that the energy penetrates three floors in the front of the building, Sam joshed to the researcher, "Does that mean I can stand in there and say 'Beam me up, Scotty,' and it'll work?"

Sam's quip aside, the Boltons are ever wary that something or somebody else is always there. In fact, it wasn't long after they moved in when a stranger came to call.

"We were here about four months," Judy said, "and a guy came in and asked if we knew that our place was haunted. I said no, but he looked me right in the eye and said, 'Oh yes, it is, and that's guaranteed!'"

That statement may have served to either raise the Boltons' awareness or spark an ongoing chain of events that has seemed to validate the stranger's assertion.

A few days after the chance encounter with the cryptic visitor, things started happening at the Boltons' combination business and residence.

Sam was minding his own business upstairs when, to his amazement, a door creaked open. Soon after, Judy had even more profound experiences.

"Sometimes," she said, "I thought I would see something. It's hard to explain. I see it, but I really don't, if you know what I mean."

I know, Judy. Trust me, I know.

Something neither of them can ever fully explain to others or themselves was an incident that took place just before and just after they went out for an evening.

One particular window in their bedroom did not stay open on its own. So, the Boltons propped it up with an antique bottle. Their little idea worked well until that one night.

They were headed out of the house when they noticed that the bottle had been flung out of the window frame. It didn't just fall, Judy said, it seemed to have been tossed into the middle of the room.

It wasn't a case of a pet knocking it out of the window, and there were no stiff breezes that evening. It couldn't have been a case of the bottle just falling and rolling across the floor into the middle of the room, because the bottle was flat on its side.

As they pondered that situation, they calmly placed the bottle back into position and went about their evening out.

When they returned, the bottle was once again astray from the window frame and in the middle of the bedroom floor!

"Another time," Judy said, "I was in the living room and a window shade just started fluttering and came out and hovered for a few seconds." The window was closed, there was no breeze, no fans in the room, and no explanation.

When she saw the hovering shade, she jokingly said she sought spirit counseling of another sort.

"I yelled to Sam, 'Hey, get me a beer!

Lights flicker regularly, and whether it's happenstance or not, whenever either of them simply "tells" the lights to stop flickering, they do.

Judy is very uncomfortable in more than one section of the antiques-packed building. She will not take a shower in the downstairs bathroom, and is hesitant to enter that room at all.

A paranormal researcher who visited Judy's shop said that he, too, felt a presence–an energy force–in that bathroom. It was not malevolent, but it was definitely centered in that room.

The building, or at least the property, is believed to have been the site of the 1755 massacre of a pioneer family by Indians.

That, among the many other dramas that have played out there over the centuries, may well be the baseline for the haunting of the otherwise charming old place.

# RESTLESS HAVEN

Some people who work there may not want to know it, but most already have heard that some of the buildings of Rest Haven, the former Schuylkill

County poorhouse, asylum, and nursing home at **Schuylkill Haven** are haunted. They would be the older buildings on the site, not the more modern section that stands next door.

Who haunts it, why they haunt it, and when their eternal imprints were made remains a mystery, but so many people have so many stories about the place that there is little doubt that the place is now the home of many restless spirits.

"Oh, yes, it is haunted," one key employee said without flinching or blinking an eye. "That's quite evident."

Speaking on conditions that her name not be published, she told of her limited personal knowledge of the hauntings.

"There's a woman dressed in white and a man dressed as a monk," she said. Both are believed by some to be harbingers of death.

Automatic doors, activated by keys or pressure, have been known to open and close on their own.

"We hear voices and footsteps, and sometimes see full apparitions," she added. Her job makes her a conversational funnel through which most of the stories must pass.

"I've heard many people, and many very honest and believable people, tell me very weird things," she noted. "It's not just employees, but visitors and guests who have no knowledge of any hauntings here have told me they have seen figures, heard sounds, or had something else strange happen to them."

As this book was being published, the stately old buildings of Rest Haven were destined to possibly become a part of the adjacent Schuylkill Campus of Penn State University.

"I can't wait to see the students come running and screaming out of there," the employee informant exclaimed.

If the stories that have circulated about what has happened in the old buildings are to be believed–and there is no reason they should not be–Rest Haven might well be, as one ghost researcher called it, "Quite possibly the most haunted place in all of Schuylkill County."

Among the most ominous of those stories involves a nurse who was reportedly passing a patient's room late at night when she saw a tall man dressed in a dark coat standing in the room. Visiting hours had expired long ago, so the nurse explained to the man that he would have to go. The nurse left the room, walked down the hall, but kept her eye on the room to make sure the man was leaving.

After a few minutes, she noticed that he hadn't left the room, so she went back. She entered the room only to find the woman dead and the black-clad man gone.

Another mystery man has been seen by many employees who took smoke breaks outside the back of the building. He has been seen gliding across the grounds, going through (literally, *going through*) a door, or as a featureless face peering through a window.

Others say they have looked into a window of the old, abandoned part of the complex and saw a group of ghostly individuals playing cards in an otherwise empty room.

The most often repeated stories involve a phantom nurse who has been spotted by several employees on several occasions and at several locations in the oldest building. She has been described as having blonde hair pulled up beneath an old-fashioned nurse's cap, and her face has never been seen. She, too, has been seen wandering the hallways, going in and out of rooms, and sometimes effortlessly passing through closed doors and interior walls.

And then, there is the "monk," or the monks. One retired caregiver said she would swear on a stack of bibles that a cloaked figure she could only describe as a monk was seen in shadowy form, lurking in corners, standing just beyond eyesight, and wandering into and out of rooms of critically-ill patients. Some accounts depict the presence of three of these monk-like men who walked together down staircases and corridors and, when someone would catch just a glimpse of them, they would disappear.

Another longtime employee reeled off these, and several other first-person encounters. What stood out in her experience was a dark shadow that would descend the staircase in the men's section of the old building. "He was wearing a long coat and a wide-brimmed hat, something like an Amishman's hat. He would be seen in silhouette or shadow going down the stairs, to where the morgue used to be. We couldn't figure that one out at all, but some said he might have been an undertaker."

Are the old buildings of Rest Haven haunted? In the opinion of one veteran worker there, "Absolutely." But, she qualified that by saying that there were few times that anything frightening ever occurred there. Even then, when a dark shadow or filmy figure was seen, the fear turned into awe in an instant.

"When I worked in that old place and saw these things, there were times I wish they would have materialized more clearly, made themselves known, and communicated with me. I would love to have known more about them. I don't think they're 'tortured souls' or anything like that. I'd like to believe that they just want to be noticed.

"I don't know what they are, or why they're here," the woman said. "But in my experience, they seem to be totally harmless. Maybe they're just the spirits of people who worked here or lived here and liked it so much they never want to leave!"

•••

## THE PHANTOM'S FETISH

"There's something or someone here, and they have a key fetish."

The words are those of Louise Ogilvie, innkeeper of The VictoriAnn Bed & Breakfast at 68 Broadway in **Jim Thorpe**.

While that declaration may be amusing at the outset, what has happened several times at the ca. 1860 building has caused Louise, a retired singer and actress, more than her share of challenges.

"Occasionally," she said, "I'll find a bedroom door locked, but it can only be locked from the inside because the only locks are dead bolts, on the inside!"

The phenomenon has caused her to find creative ways to get into the rooms. Sometimes, it's as easy as entering from an adjoining room, but she has often had to climb out one window, across a rooftop, and enter the locked room from its window.

"It's really weird," she conceded, "because there's absolutely, absolutely no way the door could be locked, except from the inside."

While that may not signal a haunting, something that a man quite familiar with the building just may.

Gene Berger has done restoration and renovation work at The VictoriAnn, and is fully convinced there is a spirit in the charming townhouse. Berger, whose own 150-year old home is haunted by a woman in a long, filmy gown, said he has felt a strong but benign energy at The VictoriAnn.

"I don't know why," he said, "but I came to call it "Alfredo."

# HAUNTED TAMAQUA

As a new millennium dawned across the globe, a ghost-hunting frenzy swept through Tamaqua as two noteworthy buildings in the bustling borough were rumored to be haunted.

The reports came from eyewitnesses of good standing in the community, and the ghost hunters came from far and wide to see what they could see, hear what they could hear, and sense what they could sense.

Teams of investigators descended on the Tamaqua Elks Lodge (B.P.O.E. Lodge No. 592) and the former P&R Railroad Station and used both equipment and instinct to "read" the two historic structures.

Their findings seemed to support the claims of several credible people who had experienced incredible and unsettling occurrences.

The Elks' building at West Broad and Nescopec Streets, was the target of a probe by members of the Pennsylvania Ghost Hunters

Society's Montour County chapter. Not long after they entered the building, they were able to conclude with little doubt in their minds that the place was haunted.

Armed with their sensitive sound, heat, light, and magnetic fields detectors, the ghost hunters discovered many "hot spots," especially on the third floor. It was there that several deaths and suicides reportedly took place during the building's century-long existence.

The ghost-tech group and an accompanying "sensitive" combined to issue preliminary observations that there are at least three active spirits, or energies, in the Elks Lodge. One inhabits a third floor men's room, another glides as a shadowy apparition through the former lodge room, and the third, a female, wanders aimlessly and endlessly down the third floor corridor.

The investigators believed that the spirits are basically benign, although some of those who swept through the building during the exercise did feel that at least one of the energy sources is so strong that it would be capable of creating pesky, poltergeist activity.

In the wake of the investigation, which garnered much publicity for the Elks and Tamaqua, the town's Historical Preservation and Tourism group organized wildly successful ghost

*The Tamaqua Elks' Lodge*

tours that wound past historical and haunted places and ended at the Elks' Lodge, which was proclaimed by the tour director as "the most haunted site in Tamaqua."

Elks' Exalted Ruler Russell Nelson tends to believe those who have detected ghostly activity at the lodge via psychic and scientific means.

"Many time, I'd be down here working and I would hear noises, banging sounds, and other things that had no explanation," he said. Doors that he was certain were locked would suddenly open. And, people would be spooked by a variety of strange happenings.

"Last year," he said, "a girl went to the bathroom on the second floor, and the water in the sink went on by itself. She was petrified."

But, is the Elks' Lodge the "most haunted

*Ghosts are said to haunt this hallway at the Tamaqua Elks' Lodge*

site" in town? Some people who have had encounters at another nearby place might mount an argument about that.

Those encounters range from the befuddling to the bewildering, and they have taken place at the Tamaqua Train Station.

Built in 1874, closed as a train depot in 1961, and abandoned in 1981, the train station is a spiritual centerpiece of the slow but steady rebirth of downtown Tamaqua.

It is also a centerpiece of spirit activity, according to contractors who have worked within its wall, on its platforms, and in tunnels that plunge into its foundation.

Others who have worked in or just passed through the station say they have had uneasy feelings that someone was shadowing them, and have even heard whisperings that seemed to utter phrases such as "Stop...please stop..." and "Help me..."

It's a no-brainer to theorize a possible baseline for a haunting at the Tamaqua Train Station. Its concourse was a waiting room for the great beyond for the dead bodies of five of the ten "Molly Maguires" who were hanged on "The Day of the Rope," June 21, 1877. The corpses were kept overnight on ice in the men's waiting room of the station until funeral arrangements were made. Two years later, the station served a similar purpose when the alleged ringleader of the Mollies, John "Black Jack" Kehoe was hanged in Pottsville and his remains were remanded to Tamaqua, where they reposed temporarily at the train station before being buried in nearby St. Jerome's Cemetery.

Are the ghosts of these men eternally ensconced in the Tamaqua Train Station?

That could be. But, Ken Smulligan, Tamaqua businessman, councilman, and president of the Tamaqua Save Our Station project during the peak of the ghost-hunting hysteria, added that there may be another, older root of hauntings.

"Tamaqua's an old Indian town," he said, "and I believe some of the buildings could have been built on sacred or ceremonial grounds. That might be the source of what has been happening, but who knows?"

Smulligan does know that he once had a firsthand experience with the ghosts of the town's two premiere haunted buildings. Oddly, though, it wasn't at the train station.

He was attending an event at the Elks Lodge when it happened. "One night we saw the silhouette of something going down the steps of the fire escape. We heard footsteps, and three of us ran down through the building to the first floor and out to the street to see who was there, and there was nobody. There were a dozen people across the street, and I knew them, and asked if they had seen anything come down the fire escape. They said no. They looked at us a little strange."

It should be noted that Ken and the other two who pursued the phantom were not thrill-seeking kids whose imaginations and senses of adventures were running amuck. They were grown men at the time.

"Lots of strange things happen in that (Elks) building," he said. "It's by far the most haunted building in Tamaqua."

But, what about the train station? "There have been many, many events there, too," Smulligan confirmed. Most seem to involve electrical circuits, tools and other items that are moved. Many could be, but rarely are, rationally explainable.

Ken Smulligan said that when the ghost hunters came to call, he wanted nothing of it. It's not that he did not approve of what they would be doing, he wanted nothing of it for another reason.

"When the paranormal people came to the station for their 'recon,'" he said, "I left them in, they stayed there for about 12 hours, but I left. That stuff gives me the willies, so I didn't stick around!"

Still, he is sensible in his thoughts about the possibility that (a) ghosts exist and (b) the Tamaqua Train Station is haunted.

"Do I believe in it? I believe that there is something more than just us, as human beings. I don't know if there are ghosts, or whatever, but there is something there."

In the wake of the extraordinary publicity the researchers' visits generated, several people revealed to Ken their own stories of eerie experiences in the old station.

As this book was going to press, the Tamaqua Train Station project was nearing completion and a reopening as a tourism and civic center. The ghost hunters' adventures were put on hold during the final phases of its rehabilitation.

"They want to come back, though," said Smulligan. "They say they hit the mother lode here."

•

*Should you be driving past St. Bertha's Cemetery along Catawissa Road in Tuscarora, beware of the ghost of a woman who might stop your car and gaze in your window. She's harmless, they say, as long as you're not the one who murdered her very long ago. Local resident Marietta Wallace said, "They claim that her killer was never found. And, if you drive up the road, just before you get to the big gates to the cemetery, your car would shut down. Then, you'll feel here ghost come by your face." ...so they claim!*

# Rebecca's...
## Fine Food & A Spirit!

Jason and Charlotte Granito knew when they purchased Rebecca's restaurant near **Orwigsburg**, that it was said to be haunted.

Jason had worked there for the previous owners several years, and he heard all the stories and experienced some of the strangeness that led to its reputation.

Now a comfortable, popular eatery, the building has a checkered past that, according to locals, includes being a house of ill repute during its days as a stagecoach stop, a lively speakeasy during Prohibition, and the site of clandestine card games.

The most infamous incident attributed to the property dates to the early 1930s, when the inn stood atop Red Church Hill surrounded by nothing more than fields and forests. It was an isolated spot then, and it was the scene of a heinous crime that shook the community at the time and may have left a permanent mark on the land upon which Rebecca's now stands.

The story has been muddled over the years, and documentation is difficult to find, but it is generally believed that on a sunny autumn morning a young couple and their toddler daughter drove to a pleasant clearing in the woods near the inn. The husband had told his wife and child that they were going for a picnic on that lovely day. Instead, and for motives forever lost in time, the man led his wife into the woods and methodically slit her throat while their daughter waited patiently in the car.

The young mother's body was buried in a shallow grave at what is now the edge of the restaurant's rear parking lot, according to what previous owners have determined.

The murderer was caught and convicted of the crime, but nothing is known about the fate of the little girl.

One longtime resident of the area did remember that the murder victim's name was Marian (or, perhaps Marion), and she was employed as a waitress in a restaurant in Reading.

And Marian, perhaps more by default than deduction, has become the ghost of Rebecca's restaurant.

Known over the years as the Hilltop Inn, the Heidelberg Inn, and Knight's Pub, it became Rebecca's in 1990 when Rebecca and Bernard Andrefski purchased it. Rebecca and Bernard, as Jason and Charlotte, knew of the tales that had been told about the ghost in the building, but were undeterred.

In a veritable explosion of publicity through the early 1990s, the ghost of Rebecca's took on a life of itself–no pun intended–as the new owners detailed their experiences in newspaper accounts throughout the region.

The Andrefskis made sweeping, positive changes to the building, and as the repairs and renovations ensued, odd things happened.

Many were of the type that come with any renovation and are sometimes too eagerly associated with the supernatural. The gas-fired fireplace fired up on its own; lights flickered and turned on and off by themselves; doors opened and closed with no human aid.

Soon, however, more profound and mysterious events began to play out. It's one thing when lights turn on and off. It's something else altogether when lights that are unplugged begin to light up.

That's exactly what greeted Bernard one day when he was working on the third floor of the building and watched in astonishment as an old neon Yuengling Beer sign began to flicker and light up, a letter at a time. He went to unplug it, only to find that it wasn't plugged in! Static electricity that ignited the neon? Perhaps. But, Rebecca chalked it up as another sign, literally, from Marian.

Another perplexing indication that the place might hold within it an energetic entity was the time when Rebecca Andrefski discovered a woman's footprints in dust that had seeped inside the second floor during an exterior sandblasting project. The footsteps, left by no one in the Andrefski family, trod across the second floor and up a staircase toward the third floor, where they disappeared.

Footsteps on the third floor were often heard by family members, and sometimes they were so loud they woke everyone in the middle of the night.

Marian–the Andrefskis naturally called their

ghost Marian–seemed to test not only the resident family but the restaurant employees as well. Just days after the business reopened, a food tray seemed to levitate from the bar and fly through the air until it landed on the floor, food strewn everywhere.

The Andrefskis were alarmed at first, but eventually grew comfortable with Marian's presence. Other than the food tray incident, the energies within the walls of Rebecca's have not done physical or psychological damage. In fact, Rebecca Andrefski eventually adjusted to Marian's presence, and considered her to be just someone who shared their home.

The restaurant stood empty and unused for nine months until the Granito family moved in and reopened it. Charlotte Granito is firmly convinced that the hiatus gave Marian some "down time," and the restaurant's resurrection served to reawaken her and rekindle her antics.

Charlotte said they were cautious about how they would deal with anything that Marian might do to make herself known. They were especially careful to not elaborate on the building's haunted reputation around their toddler, Celena.

"I thought that people were just making the stories up," Charlotte said. "I figured there might have been a shred of truth to some of it, but that most were just running with the old story. I told myself I wouldn't believe any of it until something happened to me.

"Well, something happened, and I'm a believer," she added.

What happened came quite early in the family's tenure there, and came from an unexpected source.

The parents had shielded Celena, who was not yet three years old at the time, from the details of the source and identity of the ghost that may or may not dwell in the restaurant/residence. They lightened up the story, telling their child that if she heard anything about any ghost there, it would be a ghost like "Casper," the friendly ghost.

But, one day Celena came downstairs and announced, "Mom, I think Marian is a-scared of us."

Mom was startled. "Who is what?"

"Marian, she's a-scared of us," the little girl said in her childish manner.

When Charlotte quizzed her daughter further, Celena thrust out her chest and arms, rolled her eyes high, and exclaimed, "You know, mom....Marian...the lady upstairs!"

From out of the mouth of that babe came the words that sent shivers down the spine of the mother. Still, it seemed as if the little girl was unafraid, unfazed by it all.

It wasn't long until Marian made herself known to everyone in the family. Charlotte remembered being downstairs in the bar area of the restaurant wrapping packages when, "The kitchen door swung open a little, and then shut. I thought it was just the flow of air or something. Then, it opened all the way and closed slowly. That was not a breeze. And then, all the tables on the main dining room floor shook from one end to another, as if someone was walking by."

Could that someone have been Marian, she was asked?

"Oh certainly, she replied, it was Marian."

Items have disappeared and reappeared on a regular basis at Rebecca's. The footsteps on the third floor have been heard over and over again.

Has Charlotte, the one-time skeptic, accepted the possibility that the ghost of Marian is quite real?

"Oh yes," she said without a blink. "And I'm very comfortable with her and in this place. It's like she's part of the family now. We're not at all afraid of her."

•

*It has long been believed that a ghost inhabits the abandoned Hauto Tunnel near **Lansford**. The spirit is said to be that of a worker who died during its construction.*

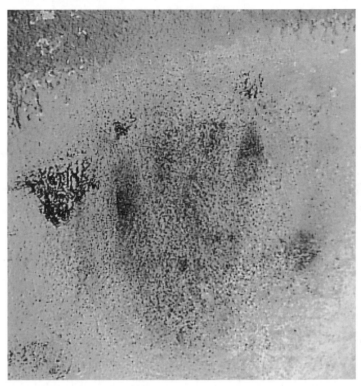

# THE GHOSTLY HAND PRINT OF CELL 17

Unquestionably, the eternal hand print of Cell 17 at the former Carbon County Prison in **Jim Thorpe** is the single most enigmatic unexplained phenomenon of Pennsylvania's anthracite "Coal Country."

The five-fingered smudge on the wall just won't go away. Neither will the lore that surrounds it.

That lore mixes historical fact and legend in a bizarre blender that has spewed out songs, stories, and speculation as to how and why the print has remained there and even who placed it there.

Be it that of Alex Campbell or Tom Fisher, the hand print is attributed to a convicted and condemned man who was linked with the notorious band of labor reformers known as the "Molly Maguires."

It is worth noting that the name given to what one historian described as an "ethnoreligious terrorist force active from the 1860s to the 1870s" was presented at that time also as the "*Mollie* Maguires," but we shall use the more accepted reference of "Molly," as in the Catholic peasant woman of County Antrim, Northern Ireland.

According to the version this writer favors, the moniker was assigned to the loosely-organized, covert, violent extension of the Ancient Order of Hibernians and honors the memory of the woman who was left as a widowed, homeless mother by an earlier band of "ethnoreligious terrorists" who murdered her husband in early 18th century Ireland, now Northern Ireland.

Myth or reality, Molly Maguire became the symbol of early struggles in her homeland and her name was carried across the sea and years and affixed to the Pennsylvania coal miners who fought their own battles against the railroad and mine barons.

The story of the Molly Maguires fills entire history books. This is a book of ghosts, legends, and lore. But, the legacy of the Mollies is pervasive in the lore of Coal Country.

In Cell 17 of the old jail in Jim Thorpe, the legacy is especially lasting– everlasting, in fact.

For years, minstrels and poets, writers and filmmakers have been drawn to the curiously romantic era and exploits of the Molly Maguires. More recently, the facts and fables of the Mollies have drawn the attention of those engaged in historical preservation and tourism.

Which leads us to the "Old Jail" in Jim Thorpe.

The facts: On "The Day of the Rope," "Black Thursday," or specifically June 21, 1877, on gallows specially built to hang four persons simultaneously, Alexander Campbell, John Donahue, Edward Kelly, and Michael Doyle were executed before a crowd of about 150 in the main cellblock of the prison. On March 28, 1878, Thomas Fisher paid the ultimate penalty on the same spot. Two more men were hanged there in 1879. And, it is known that there were at least three suicides and one inmate's murder at the prison.

With those grisly events and the stew of human dramas that often boiled over in the prison from its opening in 1871 to its closing in 1995, there are sure to be indelible energies trapped within its cellblock and dungeon.

*Which leads us to Cell 17.*

*hanged by the neck until he is dead.*

For longer than most folks in Jim Thorpe can recall, a hand print has stained a wall of that cell. Its existence has been documented in late-19th century accounts, and in 1930 the local sheriff became so perturbed by the hand print that he removed and replaced the plaster on the wall. A hand print formed at the same place on the new wall the day after it was completed.

Forensic researchers, scientists, and psychics alike have been baffled for more than a century by the hand print. More recently, tourists have joined the ranks as they stream through the prison to gawk at the gallows and ponder the print.

*Which leads us back to Alexander Campbell.*

Campbell was hanged after being convicted of conspiracy in the murder of mine superintendent John P. Jones in 1875.

On June 18, 1877, three days before "Black Thursday," *The New York Times* called Campbell and accomplice John "Yellow Jack" Donahue "thoroughly vile, with no more scruples about murdering a man than about killing an ox. They are suspected of many more crimes than those for which they are about to suffer."

Contrary to that editorial comment, Campbell and other Mollies had already become cult heroes among the Irish immigrants of Coal Country.

*Alexander Campbell*

Perhaps it was that skewed esteem that launched the legend of Alexander Campbell and the hand print.

As Campbell was being ushered out of his cell for his date with the noose, he is said to have resisted, rubbed his hand in the dirt on the floor, pressed his palm against the wall of the cell and proclaimed his innocence, shouting something like, "I am innocent! There is no proof that I am guilty! But, this hand print on this wall will never go away and will be proof forever that they have hanged an innocent man!"

*Which leads us back again to Tom Fisher.*

History and mystery simmer in an even hotter stew when Fisher's name is added to the recipe.

*Tom Fisher*

Some accounts say it was Fisher, not Campbell, who insisted on his innocence and slammed the wall to prove and preserve it.

Still more dashes of spice are added to the mix with the story that was told about a chap named Daniel Kelly (a.k.a. Manus Coll, a.k.a. "Kelly the Bum"), who is said to have contacted the prison warden the night before Fisher's execution and confessed and assured him that Fisher was indeed innocent. Although he was described as an Irish storytelling *shanachie*, and poet, "Kelly the Bum," however, was also called an "alcoholic minstrel" and "perennial prisoner," so his confession was dismissed, and Fisher was hanged.

Fisher? Campbell?

Fact? Fiction?

The story has become contradictory, confusing, convoluted and contorted over the years.

Regarding who pressed the print on the wall of Cell 17, when they did so, and if anyone actually ever did it is germane to the legend and lore of Coal Country. Sorting out the details is a daunting endeavor.

Dramatic news dispatches of what locals called the "necktie picnic" of June 21, 1877 gave readers graphic accounts of virtually every one of the last hours of the condemned men. Not one of those reports, naive as they might have been, mentions any resistance from Alexander (called "Aleck" in some stories) Campbell as he was transferred from one cell to another on his way to his fate.

After finishing his last dinner, Campbell caught a glimpse of the gallows. "A shudder ran over his face," the report said, adding that Campbell seemed a bit upset that the death-dealing framework was visible to the wives and children who visited the doomed men on their last day.

"Campbell is now quiet and docile and declares that he is innocent," the story continued, "but he pays strict attention to his devotions and says he is ready to go whenever the time comes."

As Campbell's bushy mustache was being shaved at his request, "nothing in his demeanor or language gave any indication of the least disturbance of his tranquility."

The lengthy story added that Campbell did continue to maintain his innocence, and told his captors it was hard for him to accept that he had to die for the murder of Jones, when he never knew or even saw him (he had, after all, been convicted of *conspiracy* in the murder).

Just before the noose was lifted over his head and tightened around his neck, Campbell clutched a crucifix and prayed quietly. The platform of the gallows was arranged so that two of the men faced the other two, and as they were asked for their last words, Campbell, "perfectly composed," stated clearly, "I forgive everyone. I have not an enemy in the world."

Moments later, after white hoods were placed over the men's heads, the trap doors flung open with a sickening thud and, at 10:52 a.m., June 21, 1877, the deed was done.

The bodies were left to hang for 29 minutes, and a doctor determined that Campbell had died from a broken neck.

*Which leads us to May 28, 1878.*

Thomas P. Fisher had been on the "death row" of the Mauch Chunk jail when Campbell and the three other Mollies were hanged. Further illustrating the contradictions in the reporting and assessment of the events of the day, Fisher was described in one news item as "a man of considerable intelligence" and in another as "a contemptible figure, without a gleam of intellect in his countenance."

Similarly, one report claimed that a crowd of 400 watched Fisher die, but another maintained that there was little fanfare for his execution: "The hanging of one Mollie at a time in these regions does not cause much of a ripple."

What was consistent in the stories was the sense that Fisher also went to the gibbet without a struggle. His demeanor in his final moments was solemn, serene, and repentant.

It is also interesting that in the stories about Fisher's hanging, which took place in the same jail yard and on the same gallows as Campbell's, there was no mention whatsoever about any hand print in any death row holding cell. Had Alexander Campbell actually slapped his dirty hand on the cell wall two years earlier, would not its "indelibility" had already been established, noticed, and noted? Would not the Campbell version of the hand print already been etched in legend?

*Which leads us to Cell 8.*

Cell 8?

As the hand print story has been twisted and tweaked over the years, so has the number of the cell in which the alleged event took place.

Scott Marsh, of the Lehigh Valley Ghost Hunters Society, researched the movements of the men who were executed on "Black Thursday."

"I came across a very important fact," he concluded. "Alexander Campbell, the man who supposedly left the hand print on the wall, was never held in Cell 17, where the hand print is located."

According to Marsh, "On the night before the hangings two newspapers covered the story. The *Shenandoah Herald* listed the prisoners and mentioned what cells they were in. According to this paper, Campbell was moved from cell 8 to cell 10. The *Philadelphia Evening Telegraph* also has Campbell being moved, but from cell 8 into cell 14. That news was put out at 6 p.m. and at midnight the night before the hangings. Cell 17 is nowhere near cell 10 or 14."

*Which, alas, and perhaps finally, brings us back to Tom Fisher.*

If the indelible hand print is authentic, it would almost definitely be Fisher's.

While nearly every other convicted and/or condemned Molly Maguire had an Irish surname, the name Fisher is of German extraction.

In his superb book "Lament for the Molly Maguires," author Arthur H. Lewis made a solid case that Fisher was the hand printer.

Lewis pointed out that Fisher was only half-Irish and professed that "his father was a Pennsylvania Dutchman who believed in *hexerei*..." That, he reasoned, also would have made Fisher a believer, and possibly prone to place a curse or hex on the cell, the prison, and his accusers.

Still, there are doubts. As have others, Lewis wrote that Fisher placed his right hand on the cell wall, and that hand print is the one that remained. Photographs published in newspapers showed the right-hand print.

The hand print on the wall of Cell 17 today is most definitely a left-hand print.

Lewis confirmed that the hand print was still on the wall in his 1964 book, but failed to note the digital discrepancy.

Fact? Fiction?

Campbell? Fisher?

Does it matter?

What matters is that the hand print has added a tempting touch of mystery to the history of the Molly Maguires and Coal Country.

*Which leads us to the ghost stories.*

Several people have spoken of having eerie encounters as they toured the Old Jail Museum, now a very popular attraction set inside the building that is on the National Register of Historic Places.

Any spirits that dwell in the cells and dungeon of the jail seem to be troubled, but not troublesome. Melancholy voices have been heard at various spots by various people.

A woman's voice has been heard to echo softly, "I'm too late...I'm too late." Another pleads for the passerby to "Go away...I want to be alone."

The prospect of a haunted jail drew the attention of the Philadelphia Ghost Hunters Alliance, whose members made their first trip to Jim Thorpe in October, 2003, to conduct what PGHA president Lew Gerew called "the first-ever scientific inquiry into potential haunting activity at the Carbon County Jail in Jim Thorpe."

The investigation utilized the basic tools of modern "ghost hunting," an electromagnetic field detector, infrared thermometer, night vision scope, motion detectors, and still and video cameras.

The equipment was carried or set up throughout the jail, and in the three-hour foray the sophisticated gear yielded few anomalies.

However, other sensors provided many intriguing findings, leading Gerew to conclude, "There were many suggestions of paranormal activity in this preliminary investigation."

Those sensors that caused the nocturnal visitors to stop, look, and listen intently were the sensors of their own minds–usually the most responsive receivers of all.

A shuffling sound in Cell 23...A creaking noise near the gallows....A blue light glowing in the solitary confinement "dungeon"...The soft sound of "booted footsteps"....These and other phenomena peppered the probers' experiences that night.

Is the Old Jail haunted?

Tom and Betty Lou McBride rescued the old jail from an ignoble fate when they purchased it in 1996 and opened it for public tours. As the keepers of the key to the jail, they, if anyone, should be able to answer that question.

"But," Tom McBride kidded, "my name is 'Thomas,' as in 'doubting Thomas.'"

Thus, he is on the fence when it comes to his personal belief that ghostly energies swirl within the walls of the gothic structure.

Still, a preponderance of evidence and testimonies have even "doubting Thomas" teetering toward belief.

"When we opened the jail for tours," he said, "we never thought of any ghostly aspects to it. But, as the tours started, people would come up to us afterward and tell us they got goosebumps, or felt as if they were being pushed, or felt a strange sensation. At first, we shrugged it off. But then, we noticed a pattern emerging."

The McBrides began to keep an informal log of the times and places tourists reported their unsettling feelings. That log is now a file folder more than an inch thick with handwritten notes and letters from visitors.

One particular place emerged as a "hot spot" of activity, according to Tom.

Although he disclosed to this writer the specific (and, perhaps, unexpected) area where the most intense feelings have been sensed, he asked that the location not be disclosed. "I wouldn't want someone to be predisposed, and go there anticipating something." He feels that it's more valuable (and this writer agrees) to continue to register the visitors' experiences, note the locale, and see if the pattern continues.

It also makes a visit to the old jail all the more adventurous to the would-be ghost hunter. It adds a great deal of mystery to the history of the jail.

In general terms, the reports fed back to the McBrides and their tour guides over the years have included folks feeling as if they met a resistance, a "wall of air," as one described it, as they walked in certain sections of the jail. Another individual, trained as an emergency medical technician, felt her pulse rate race and then back off as she walked through a particular area.

Students in school groups have felt as if someone was placing a hand softly on their shoulder. A woman once told Tom that she felt as if she was walking uphill–on the flat floor of the jail.

The McBrides' own niece, visiting from Ohio, even disclosed that she had an unwelcome feeling in that undisclosed "hot spot."

Tom and Mary Lou afforded the girl the opportunity to return to that spot "after hours." She was left alone there, and when she emerged after a lengthy time, she said she felt as if she had actually communicated with the spirit that resides there.

Tom is quite aware of the confusion and controversy that surrounds the left hand/right hand, Campbell/Fisher, Cell 8/Cell 17 questions at the old jail. He indicated that it seems likely that Fisher was the more logical candidate as the source of the hand print, and that the thumb print that marks the smudge as a left hand only surfaced relatively recently. For many years, the print was more a palm and four fingers, which made it inconclusive as to it being a right or left hand.

The sheer height of the print on the cell wall illustrates that whoever placed it there was at least six feet tall. McBride has discovered that Campbell was 6'2" tall, but there are no references to Thomas Fisher's height.

As for the cell number, McBride referred to one "history" book that placed Alexander Campbell, one of the condemned quartet of "Black Thursday" in three differently-numbered cells. Even the contemporary newspaper stories contradicted one another, as previously noted.

*Which leads me to Charles Sharp and James McDonnell.*

I say leads *me* to those men because I will now dare to add other individuals into the mix–other

Molly Maguires who met their maker on the gallows of the Mauch Chunk jail nearly ten months after Thomas Fisher was hanged.

I will also assert that I believe the energy, or more properly the energies that inhabit the old jail are likely to be those generated in the final moments in the lives of Charles Sharp and James McDonnell.

Little is known Sharp (or "Sharpe") or McDonnell (or "McDonald"), but the details of the events on the day of their deaths are spine-chilling and sickening.

If everything you read on these pages indeed added mystery to history, then the Sharp and McDonnell story will add misery to the mystery.

Theirs was the third-to-last Molly Maguire "necktie picnic," and by the time of their executions on January 14, 1879, the public and the press had apparently grown weary of the Molly Maguire trials and hangings.

They had both been arrested in 1877 for the 1863 murder of George Smith in Audenried. They were convicted of the murder in April, 1878, partly on testimony by "Kelly the Bum."

Based on what happened on the day of their hangings, an argument could be made, but has not been until now, that they are as likely candidates for placing the hand print on the cell wall as anyone else.

If neither made the hand print (Sharp was described as "below medium height"), it is still entirely conceivable that it is their energies and a vortex of potent energies that was imprinted at the old jail on that cold day in January that remains there and accounts for the building's haunting.

As they suffered in their grim, dark, damp eight-by-thirteen feet cells, their lawyer was hard at work seeking legal remedies and clemency. He had already won one reprieve for the men, but by early January, 1879, time was running out.

On the 13th, the attorney did make one final trip to Harrisburg to seek another reprieve from Gov. John F. Hartranft. He was shocked to find that the governor was in Washington on business.

But, when the next day dawned and Sharp and McDonnell were hours away from hanging, the lawyer secured the stay of execution.

He immediately sent a telegram to Mauch Chunk and begged the telegraph operator to rush it to the jail and halt the execution.

The message reached the telegraph office at 10:37 a.m. Charles Sharp and James McDonnell had been taken out of their cells at 10:25 a.m., and were being prepared for their deaths.

The telegraph office was at the train station at the foot of Broadway, about a third of a mile away. Operator Philip Laudenslager, fully aware of the life-or-death urgency of the missive, dashed out of the office and ran at full speed up the snowy, icy hill of Broadway to the jail.

Already at the locked front door of the building were the men's hysterical wives. Mrs. Sharp had been there for hours, weeping, screaming, and begging for her beloved's life to be spared. Sheriff Jacob Raudenbush had grown accustomed to and tired of her banging on the door and pitiful wailing. If he and the jailers could hear it, no doubt Sharp could, as well. It must have devastated him.

Mrs. McDonnell and her daughter arrived just before her execution and joined Mrs. Sharp at the front door.

One account of the day said that Laudenslager managed to rush from the telegraph office to the jail in about four minutes. That would have placed his arrival there at 10:41 a.m.

He joined the women, shrieking and beating on the door. He clutched in his hand the document that would, at least temporarily, save the men's lives.

It is said that the sheriff noted the more intense banging and caterwauling and told those at the gallows to ignore it, that it was just Mrs. Sharp again.

# Coal Country Ghosts, Legends, and Lore

As the sobbing wives and the young man with the reprieve papers in his fist were ignored, the trap doors opened and Charles Sharp and James McDonnell were hanged at 10:52 a.m. The deed done, Sheriff Raudenbush strolled to the front door, opened it, and found the telegraph operator physically exhausted and spiritually spent. Mrs. Sharp's grief and rage were uncontrollable. She lunged at the sheriff, but was quickly subdued. The sizable crowd that had gathered on the street below the front door of the jail was ordered to disperse, and did so amid murmurs of disillusion and discontent.

"The spectacle," the *Reading Eagle* reported, "was one to touch the heart of the most sordid."

The incident drew the wrath of the newspaper writers of the day and of later authors. The *New York World* called the episode "a disgrace to public justice in the state of Pennsylvania."

In his "Making Sense of the Molly Maguires," author Kevin Kenny called the governor's casual approach to the matter of the reprieve "negligence" and Sheriff Raudenbush's actions "unseemly hasty."

Anthony Bimba wrote in his book, "The Molly Maguires," that the matter was "shady."

It is well known by those who investigate ghostly occurrences that extreme trauma, not limited to death, can create the "baseline" for a haunting.

Imagine the horrid events of that grim January morning as you stand in front of the old jail. If you are sensitive, if all conditions are right, you

*"Sharp's contortions were fearful.*
*He drew his body up, and then shivered so*
*that the frame of the gallows shook."*
–Reading Eagle, *January 14, 1879*

may hear the thumping of frantic fists and the echoing sounds of shrieks and sobs. Maybe you will hear the clunk of the gallows trap door, the whoosh of the bodies as they fall, and a dull crack as the knot of the noose snaps a man's neck.

That the hand print in Cell 17 is Charles Sharp's or James McConnell's is as likely as any other scenario. That the ghostly energy there is the collective forces of the hanged men, their wives, and even the frenzied telegraph operator seems entirely probable.

Even though he owns the jail and treasures its history and its mysteries, Tom McBride is as bewildered and beguiled as anyone when it comes to the ever-present hand print and the ever-mounting body of evidence that the place is haunted by the anguished and angry ghosts of the men many people believe were unjustly executed so long ago.

In *Terrorism as Heritage: How the Molly Maguires Became a Tourist Attraction*, Philip Jenkins, Distinguished Professor of History and Religious Studies at Penn State wrote that to many people, rightly or wrongly, the old jail in old Mauch Chunk–the place of the deaths of those Mollies–was "their Calvary...where innocents were martyred for their social activism and their persecuted ethnicity."

# A Gathering of Spirits

Bob Ewashko and Sheila O'Neil are typical of many folks who relocated to **Jim Thorpe** to rebuild their lives, rediscover their dreams, and reconnect with themselves as they helped to reinvent the town.

Their dream was to operate a bed and breakfast inn while still pursuing their full-time jobs. After a lengthy search of many properties in many towns, they bought a property at 40 West Broadway.

The most notable resident of the home was David Jarvis Pearsall, the personal secretary of Mary Packer Cummings and a man who held positions of power and prestige in old Mauch Chunk and beyond.

The conversion to what would become the Gilded Cupid B&B would be a challenge. Its previous tenants had, shall we say, a less lofty attitude and little appreciation for the architectural and historical attributes of the building. Details will be skipped, but suffice to say there are still marks from motorcycle kick stands that were pressed into the hardwood floors of the parlor.

That ignoble era of the house has spawned many inaccurate and exaggerated rumors and wild stories about the place.

According to Sheila, the real story–the real haunting of 40 West Broadway is more awe-inspiring than the lurid tales that have been told.

The extensive remodeling of the 140-year old home was centered in what is now the dining room of the B&B. It was once Pearsall's office, and its dark chestnut woodwork and heavy doors with huge iron hinges and latches still suggest a very masculine atmosphere.

That masculinity has all been tempered a bit by soft and subtle design touches, but it was in the dining room where Bob and Sheila had their introduction to the energies that inhabit the home.

"Up to that point, I felt that I was a seer of the next dimension," Sheila said. "But Bob was a non-believer."

Sheila is also a gourmet cook, fiercely proud of her culinary skills.

Early in the remodeling and restoration phase of the old home, Sheila was on a ladder in the parlor, staining woodwork. "Bob came in and asked me what I was burning on the stove," she remembered. "Well, that is something you don't say to an accomplished chef!

"So, I turned around and looked into the dining room and swirling around was the energy of the ghosts!"

Bob thought it was smoke at first, but had to admit that there was no accompanying smoky aroma, and it was something unlike anything he had seen before.

"I can only think that the spirits were happy that we were bringing the house back to its dignity," Sheila said. "I get a feeling back from this house."

She feels that it is not just their B&B, but the entire town of Jim Thorpe, that is enchanted.

"There is an energy in these mountains and from these mountains," she maintained. "Some people suggest that geologically, when you have two mountains coming together dramatically and they are separated by water, vortices of energy are created."

Sheila recalled stories of Native American shamans who were said to have gathered on the hillside that rises suddenly in back of the house and pointed out that a stream actually flows beneath the building.

"I believe the energy field that is here is real," she said. "It's throughout the community." She feels that the energy has built up over the years and is continually refreshed and regenerated by the people and events in Jim Thorpe.

Sheila has put her time and efforts where her sentiments are. At the time of this writing, she was president of the Mauch Chunk Historical Society, and deeply committed to both the past and the future of her adopted home town.

She believes the richness of Irish beliefs and folklore attached to the area by some of its earliest European settlers has also contributed to the classic spiral of energy that washes over Jim Thorpe.

Bob and Sheila said several guests have told them they feel an energy–a comfortable energy–at the Gilded Cupid.

"I feel that it's a gathering of spirits," she said, with a smile–a comfortable smile–on her face.

# PHANTOM OF THE (MAUCH CHUNK) OPERA

Actors and actresses scurry about, the sound of their footsteps creaking across worn, wooden floors.

Carpenters and painters busily bang and clang away backstage, building sets and repairing equipment.

Light and sound technicians tweak and test their systems, their labors obvious as lights dim and flicker and noises bellow from speakers.

A solitary singer rehearses in the balcony, her sweet melodies echoing softly in the auditorium.

These are what one would expect to see and hear as a theatrical production company prepares for a show. These are *not* what would be expected to be seen and heard in an *empty* theater.

They are samplings of what has been experienced by several credible people over the years in the Mauch Chunk Opera House in **Jim Thorpe**.

Built in 1881 as a multipurpose community center with a farmers market on the first floor and a concert and meeting hall on the second, the Opera House has seen its share of shining stars and faded glory.

From a topnotch vaudeville house to a movie theater to a warehouse for a handbag manufacturer, the noble building has had a storied past. In 1975, the Mauch Chunk Historical Society chose dignity over demolition and purchased the building.

It has since become a venue for cultural events, both scheduled and unscheduled.

Several performers, producers, and patrons have been treated to spooky spontaneous outbursts that have led many people to believe the Opera House has a resident phantom.

"Oh yes, it certainly does," said Sandy Reese. "It roams around, it floats around. It moves things."

Sandy should know. She lives across the street from the Opera House and has often stood candlelight vigil inside the theater under a full moon, hoping the phantom will reveal itself.

She has a special feeling for, and about the building. Sandy is first vice-president of the Mauch Chunk Historical Society and the events coordinator of the Opera House.

"A lot of times," she continued, "you can hear it upstairs, or backstage. You can feel its presence."

Sandy is careful to call the Opera House ghost "it," as there is no firm baseline from which its presence could be traced. Sandy said there is an unconfirmed story that a man died inside when it was a movie house, but knows nothing more than that.

What she does know is that several patrons, with no knowledge of the suspected haunting of the building, have merged from shows and told her that they felt there was a strong energy circulating inside.

"There was a TV crew here one time," she added, "and the cameraman had to stop the taping and take a break because he felt an overpowering feeling. I knew we were the only ones in the building. He even said that at one point while he was taping he saw someone peeping between the curtains. Funny thing was, though–nothing showed up when he played the tape back!"

# THE PROTECTORS

Novelist John O'Hara came to call his hometown of **Pottsville** "Gibbsville," and he portrayed it as a town in its death throes, smothered by the closure of coal mines and cold minds.

O'Hara, of course, wrote fiction. The charm of the city lies deep within the hearts and souls of its people, not deep within the shafts of the mines that lace the hills around it.

Those hills have been alive with the sound of music in Gibbs/Pottville since 1979, when the Schuylkill County Council for the Arts occupied one of the most handsome and historic mansions in the city.

# Coal Country Ghosts, Legends, and Lore

From the National Historic District downtown, Mahantongo Street ascends on a steady grade as its storefronts turn into rowhomes, the rowhomes into townhouses, and the townhouses into stately rows of Georgian and Victorian manses where coal barons once resided.

Mahantongo seems to never really reach the elusive summit of the hill it climbs. Block by block, cross streets climb and plummet along the severe slopes until the street finally levels off. At about that point, at 1440 Mahantongo, is the Yuengling Mansion.

With 20 rooms and its Jacobean Tudor architecture, the mansion would be just another "Millionaire's Row" relic but for its familiar past and functional present.

It was built in 1913 by Frank D. Yuengling, the third president of the brewery that still bears his family name.

If Frank could return for a look, he would probably be comfortable there. The mansion is not so much restored, but maintained. It is a maze of ample chambers that now serve for rehearsals, recitals, and exhibits. It is spectacular.

And, some people believe, it is haunted.

Missi Boyer is one of them. She is the arts director there, and she has good reason to think that previous residents may still be there, protecting their prized old home.

It didn't start that way, however. Missi was in the ranks of the nonbelievers when she started her job there.

At the very outset, she heard stories of doors that opened on their own and strange, unexplainable sounds that had been heard.

"People would tell me the building was haunted," she said. "I would tell them, 'yeah, yeah, it's an old building, and things could happen in it."

One individual went as far as describing the spirit as that as a powerful man, alluding perhaps to David Yuengling himself.

What Missi would experience led her in a different direction.

"I was hanging a show in 2002," she said, "and there were 102 paintings. We had to use walls we never used before. We had to put nails in the wall for some of them, which we hate to do because of the historic nature of the house.

"I was putting a nail in a wall in the hallway going up to the third floor, where the maids' quarters were when the Yuengling family lived there, and where the children would have spent a lot of time.

"I was putting the third nail in the wall and I heard footsteps climbing up the stairs. Then, I heard a door slam at the top of the steps. I thought it was my assistant, so I yelled to her, figuring it was her going up the stairs. It turned out that she was on my computer, down the hall, in the opposite direction."

It was at that point when Missi had her ethereal epiphany.

"I quickly ran into her and told her that the ghost was not a man, it was a woman and a child. I just had that feeling, if you know what I mean."

Not only was it a female spirit, it also had, as Missi called it, "an attitude." She believed it manifested itself because someone was hammering a nail into the pristine wall.

"Many unexplained things happen here," Missi continued. "We get a lot of doors slamming, windows opening and closing, things like that. Much of it seems to be things that a child's ghost would do."

Several others who work, practice, or perform in the Council of the Arts building have had experiences.

"I have a theory," Missi offered. "I think the women of the house would be more concerned about the building, about putting a nail in a wall, and things like that. I don't know why, but I really believe there are ghosts of a woman and a little girl here. They're just protecting the place."

# BUTTERFLIES, BEES, AND BOO!

For boxing fans, it is a genuine historic site. For Muhammad Ali fans, it is a shrine. For travelers seeking truly unique accommodations, it is a five-star find.

For the pages of a ghost story book, it is a classic.

The Butterfly & Bee Bed & Breakfast, at what locals call "Dead Man's Curve Hill" along Sculps Hill Road near **Deer Lake**, is owned by Pottsville native, Reading resident, and world-renowned black belt karate champion George Dillman and his wife, Kim.

Dillman and Ali became training mates and

friends in the early 1970s when Ali started working out at the former mink farm in the woods atop Sculps Hill.

The history of Ali's camp is colorful. Past and future ring champs–Leonard, Holmes, Tyson among them–trained there. Everybody who was anybody–Sinatra, Presley, Warhol, Sammy Davis Jr., and Michael Jackson among them–made pilgrimages there. And, at least one of Ali's confidantes, Drew "Bundini" Brown, may still be in camp there.

"I really do believe Bundini Brown's spirit is there," Dillman said. "And, I think it cares about who stays in his old cabin."

Interestingly, Brown was described by one writer as "Ali's longtime shadow" and the fighter's "ghostwriter." It was Brown who came up with the buzz phrase that described Ali's boxing style: "Float like a butterfly, sting like a bee."

Given that fact, and given the name of Dillman's B&B that now occupies the old training camp, it would seem only appropriate that Brown's leftover energy remains on the property.

Dillman has seen what he described as a "spooky figure, a kind of smoky form" in Bundini's cabin.

"I knew from the beginning that there were spirits there," he said of his B&B. "Construction workers and repairmen have told me of many weird experiences," he added. The ghost, or ghosts, at the B&B B&B have been described as more mischievous than malicious, although at least two guests have scurried from their cabin-the Bundini cabin-after encounters with the entities.

"We've had three caretakers here," Dillman said, "and each of them had stories about the ghosts."

At this writing, Daniel Blatt was caretaker, and although he is skeptical about the existence of ghosts *anywhere*, he cannot deny what has gone on *there*.

"I think something's happening here," he said. The *here* he spoke of was his own residence, a camp structure called "The Chalet."

"When you're here all alone and you hear footsteps upstairs or doors creaking open, and you think there's somebody else here but you know there isn't, you become convinced there's something haunting the place," Blatt said. He also confirmed the numerous reports of strange happenings in the cluster of cabins across the road. "Oh yeah," he sighed, "there are ghosts around here."

That might be an understatement.

Dillman provided the names of more than a dozen guests who have told him that they have gone a few rounds with the ghosts of the Butterfly & Bee.

One, who did not want his name mentioned, said he was once awakened in the middle of the night by a softly glowing figure that shuffled past his bed. "What woke me up was the cold. It was early July, and about 80 degrees outside. All of a sudden, the temperature dropped to what must have been around freezing. It got so cold so fast that I woke up, and saw the glowing form glide past the bed. When it disappeared, the room got warm again...and I managed to get back to sleep!"

Ron Baddorf, an Arizona resident who has attended several of Dillman's martial arts camps at the B&B, said he was once vexed by a balky door in his cabin, and after trying to forcefully open it, he gave up. Having heard the tales of Brown's ghost there, he tried another tack and gently said, "All right now, Bundini, stop messing around..."

The door gently swung open.

Siobhan Knuttel comes from her home on Cape Cod to attend and assist at the karate camps, and on one occasion, she was in the kitchen setting up for the day, making coffee, etc., when, as she said, "I had the distinct feeling that someone was following me. I heard someone milling about around the fireplace.

"I went out to tell them that the coffee was

ready, but there was no one there. I heard the same sound and went out a total of three times. I was sure I wasn't alone, but I was also sure there was nobody else there, if you know what I mean. I guess it was the ghost."

Nevada resident Ed Lake was also left with the very strong impression that he was not by himself when he occupied Cabin No. 7.

"Unbeknownst to me when we first went to stay there," he said, "there was common knowledge there that the cabin was supposed to be 'haunted.'

"I walked into a door and could feel a presence right away. There was something different in that one cabin. I had been in other cabins, but this one definitely had a different feel to it.

"All of a sudden, as I was trying to figure out what exactly was there, the door slammed shut, as if it was a sign."

Lake stayed in the cabin four nights, and every one of his senses was titillated by the presence. He caught a whiff of a tobacco aroma, heard phantom laughter, and caught glimpses of shadows that darted just beyond his eyesight.

"Actually, though," he said, "it was a very pleasant experience there. At one point, I even started to talk to the ghost. But, he never talked back!"

# Embracing the Energies of
# The Smith Mansion

When Gary Senavites and Michael Cheslock purchased the Smith Mansion in 1986, they fully accepted the realities and responsibilities of owning one of the most handsome homes in **Mahanoy City**.

The realities included pouring untold sums of love, labor, and money into its restoration. The responsibilities included tolerating and tending to the needs of its tenants.

No, the Smith Mansion is not an apartment building and no, Senavites and Cheslock are not landlords.

But yes, there seem to be tenants in the marvelous Victorian home—eternal tenants.

Michael Cheslock thinks of the house as a "living entity" and feels his obligation is to maintain it with dignity so it will remain healthy long after he is gone.

To that end, he and Gary have fashioned what amounts to what he calls a "mini-museum of the Smith family" that honors the family that resided there from when it was built in 1908 to the early 1970s.

It was the home of John Smith, who was a hotelier, merchant, and bank president in Mahanoy City in the early twentieth century. He and his wife Anna raised 11 children there, and Michael believes the spirit of one of those children may still linger.

He said that as he and Gary were about to move into the big house on the "Pottsy" hill, they were discussing their move with a psychic.

"We were told that we would end up as caretakers of the house, that was what our position would be," Michael said.

While that seemed somewhat apocryphal, it might well have been accurate.

"Shortly after that," Michael continued, "I had the feeling that the house didn't really belong to me, and that it still belonged to the Smiths and they were fortunate enough to find me. And, in finding them, I found something special in the house that I wouldn't have otherwise."

It seemed as if the walls of the house were, not just figuratively, talking to him. He recalled several puzzling incidents.

Michael's sanctuary in the house is the signature "tower room" that rises high above Main and Spruce streets and offers a sweeping view of the town, the mountains, and the mines. It is his meditation and prayer room.

"I was up in the tower room praying. While I was praying, I was also thinking about the Smith family. There's a little bedroom next to the tower room, all at once I heard a weird sound come from that room. It was a groaning, gasping sound. There was nobody else in the house at the time, and I walked down the steps with the hair sticking up on my arms.

"Another time, I was going down the back staircase and I got to the bottom to wake up my partner. I yelled, 'Gary...Gary...' And, he didn't answer. The next thing I knew, I heard these girls' voices–it sounded like more than one girl–chiming '*Gary...Gary...Gary...*'"

Michael was certain that Gary hadn't awakened and mockingly returned the call. He knew there were no girls nor anyone at all in the house other than he and Gary. And, he knew the sound was coming from within the house, not the outside.

The bedroom that adjoins the tower room was, as Michael has been told, occupied by one particular Smith daughter who had, shall we say, special needs.

He has come to believe, and almost hope, that the energy of that little girl's life has been imprinted indelibly in the house.

"I see the house as having something that is part of the family that *was* there and maybe even the daughter that may *still be* there," he said.

"She's doing in the house what I would like to do if I lived there forever. I think she's embracing the new occupants because the new occupants are embracing her."

## Person to Person, Patch to Patch....
# Coal Country Ghosts

*In the quest for true ghost stories in Schuylkill and Carbon counties, many people offered tales of their own experiences in the past and in the present. What follows is a sampling of these individuals' recollections and reports, as well as other stories gathered in the patch towns, mountains, and valleys of Coal Country.*

•

"We'd be sitting for dinner and we'd see somebody come past the window,"said George Shuler of his childhood home in **Llewellyn**. "But, nobody ever knocked at the door.

"One day my mother was vacuuming and she saw an old lady walk past the window. She got up, went to the door, and there was nobody there, not on the porch, the walk, anywhere. And, it definitely was an old lady, so she couldn't have gotten away that quickly. I saw her, my mother saw her, I even have a friend who saw her.

"Now, I'm a Christian, and I don't exactly understand where it comes to play in all of this, but I know I've seen these things, and they're around."

•

A story has been told for several decades of the ghostly drag racer of Route 209 somewhere between **Pottsville** and **Tamaqua**.

Rick Bugera, founder and president of the Berks County Paranormal Association, tracked down the story:

"Back in the 1960s and 1970s," he said, "drag racing was very popular among certain people in Schuylkill County. There was a rivalry between the racers from Tamaqua and Pottsville.

"They used to race on a quarter-mile stretch of Route 209, closer to Pottsville. My research into this indicates that it is not the existing Route 209, but the old Route 209.

"One year, on July 27th, a drag racer had a very unfortunate and lethal accident. It is said that if you are standing along that quarter-mile stretch of roadway, you will hear an engine rev, tires squeal, and then see a car go flying past you, burst into flames, fly into the woods, and then vanish into thin air."

•

Old-timers in **Auburn** still tell tales of the ghost that haunted the pump house at the old train station on Bear Creek Street.

It was said that a man hanged himself in the building and when conditions were just right, passersby would see his shadowy, spectral form dangling from the rafters.

•

The Cafe is the name of a comfortable family restaurant on Route 61 at **Deer Lake**. And, its proprietor and her employees blame anything unusual that happens there on a ghost they call "Nick."

Not much is known about Nick, other than he worked at the restaurant in the 1950s or 1960s and was struck by a car and killed on the highway in front of what was known as "Phaon's" at the time.

"Ever since then," the current owner said, "things have happened. Pots fly in the kitchen, pans drop on their own, and there are strange thumps, bumps, and bangs." She said one of her cooks was even hit on the head by a seemingly "flying" frying pan!

Whenever the activity in The Cafe reaches a

peak, somebody will simply say "Nick-Nick, knock it off," and the thumps, bumps, and bangs will cease.

•

Some people there are understandably uncomfortable talking about it, but it seems as if everyone knows the story about the ghost that is said to roam in and around a nursing home just outside **Tremont**.

Gwynn McCabe heard the story from longtime employees right after she graduated from high school and went into training there.

"They came up to me and asked if anyone had told me about the little boy," she said. "Well, I cautiously told them no. They told me that an older boy was riding on the road where the nursing home was built.

"They said any time someone is close to passing away, or has passed away, there would be a cool breeze down the hallway, the curtains would ruffle, and the little boy's spirit could be seen."

Some patients, including a retired doctor, have reported seeing the little boy in their rooms. Could it be dementia? Delusions? Is it all an urban legend of a familiar type? Perhaps.

Still, Gwynn and others who know the story continue to receive signs and sensations that lead them to believe that the little boy's spirit may well come to call every once in a while.

•

There is a similar hesitancy on the part of some at the News-Item newspaper office in **Ashland** to speak of that building's apparent haunting.

One employee, who spoke on the condition that her name not be published, did comment on the occurrences in the Main Street office.

"There have been a few odds things happening," she said. Doors opening, computer glitches, things like that.

"One girl who was in editorial swore that when she went out one night there was something in the hallway, and she just ran. She left."

That's "left," as in quit her job. She told others at the office that seeing what she believed to be a ghost was a major contributor in her decision to leave.

"We do hear footsteps, upstairs in the abandoned apartment," the woman continued. "The people left quite abruptly-so quickly, in fact, that they left all their stuff up there!

"I think there is a presence in the building, but it doesn't bother me at all. It can't hurt me."

•

Along Church Road near **Laurytown** and

**Rockport** is a desolate, decrepit, and desecrated old graveyard that has been known for decades locally as "The Haunted Cemetery."

It is perhaps sadly true, however, that it has been haunted more by vandals than by ghosts. One gentlemen theorized that they started to call the former St. Joseph's church graveyard "haunted" to keep people out, but it seemed to have the opposite effect.

In an area once called "Grog Hollow," the old cemetery hasn't had a burial in many, many years. On its vine-twisted, weed-infested, pitted grounds is still visible the faint outline of where the church stood before it fell to an arson's torch in 1966. The parish was closed and merged with St. Nicholas in Weatherly.

The ghosts of this particular "haunted cemetery" seem to haunt only the imaginations of thoughtless seekers who have strewn the grounds with trash, bottles, and cans that once held another kind of spirits.

Still, there are some who say they have witnessed shadowy forms and glowing figures gliding between the broken and battered tombstones there.

Parents once warned their children that if they walked on that cemetery and stepped on a grave, a bony hand might rise from the soil, grab their legs, and pull them under. One woman said she had heard that admonition, and when she was walking through the graveyard as a child, she stepped on a grave and actually felt a force from the soil clasping her ankle. It was the briers from a wild mulberry bush!

The cemetery is also the epicenter of other

local legends, including a Coal Country version of the "hook man" and the ever-popular "couch"-a seat-like rock formation that will prove fatal to anyone who sits upon it three times-or so it is believed

•

Should you visit the Liberty Pub on Broad Street in **Beaver Meadows**, you may see what Marilyn Fisher has seen–three ghosts.

Friend of pub owner Frank Dreitlein, Marilyn said, "They don't hurt anybody, they don't do anything wrong. They just appear and disappear."

She described the phantoms as two pale shadows and one that is much darker. Although none has done anything other than materialize from time to time, she feels the dark shadow is more sinister. Both she and Frank believe at least one of the spirits may be that of a former owner, who died in the building.

•

The town of **Port Clinton**, nestled in the Schuylkill River Gap, could be considered to be the gateway to both the Pennsylvania Dutch Country of Berks County to the south and the Coal Country of Schuylkill County to the north.

Named after New York Gov. DeWitt Clinton, who was instrumental in the building of the Erie Canal, Port Clinton itself was in a pivotal position as a port along the Schuylkill Canal in the nineteenth century. When railroads supplanted canals as major haulers of "black diamonds" from the coal mines to the commercial markets, both the Pennsylvania and Reading rail lines passed through Port Clinton. The town's role as a rail hub was more recently reinforced when the Reading & Northern Railroad built its offices, shops, and yard there.

A legacy of Port Clinton's past is the ca. 1845 Union House, once and still a boarding house, bar, and restaurant. The property honors that legacy with such touches as serving Yuengling Beer, heating its guest rooms with coal in locally made stoves, gracing the rooms with Pennsylvania Dutch quilts, placing a 26-ton, ca. 1945 Lehigh Valley on its porch, and using a recipe that originated there in the 1800s for its famous crab cakes.

A building so old and so active over the years must certainly have its share of ghosts. And, according to innkeeper Herman Baver, it just might.

"We hear weird noises," he said as he admitted that the 60 shutters on the windows and the tin on the roof might contribute to some of those sounds. "But, there's more," he added.

"Waitresses and some customers all reported hearing the old screen door open up as if someone was coming in, but nobody ever did," Baver said. He also said several employees report a general uneasiness-the sense that they are not alone-in some nonpublic spaces in the Union House.

Independent observations by a psychic who made an unannounced visit to the Union House revealed his belief that there are two ghostly presences within and outside the walls of the building.

"People there should keep a lookout for an older woman with her hair woven into a tight bun," he noted. Preferring to remain anonymous, the psychic felt the woman was likely, in life, a waitress there around the turn of the twentieth century.

"I even felt as if the name 'Beatrice' may mean something," he continued. I don't think she died there, but she suffered some sort of traumatic experience there and her energy was deposited there."

But, that's not all.

"There's also, I feel, a very strong energy that is a little less gentle. Luckily, that masculine spirit is outside the building. I don't know who it is, or why it remains, but the man's ghost seems agitated or angry. As just energy, though 'he' can do no harm to anyone or anything. But, there's a good bet those who are sensitive will certainly feel his presence there."

Although a steady flow of traffic travels through Port Clinton on Route 61, and although that highway has obliterated much of the nineteenth century configuration of the landscape there, another story of another haunted spot near Port Clinton still resounds in the Schuylkill Gap.

It is said that a young woman was murdered on a covered bridge that once spanned the river just south of Port Clinton, near the Berks-Schuylkill county line. In the early 1900s, stories persisted that on the anniversary of the crime, December 6, the ghost of the girl appeared and the murder was reenacted on the covered bridge.

In 1928, a group of young people from the area decided to go ghost hunting at the bridge. Their expedition was recounted by one of the young men in the party in the pages of a publication of the day.

The adventurers made their way to the bridge early in the evening and were prepared to wait as long as it might take until something would happen.

Their patience was rewarded, as reported:

*All at once we heard chains rattle on the bridge, as if being dragged.*

*After a few moments this stopped and a we heard a noise like a horse walking around on the bridge and then back again,*

*A man's rough voice was then heard followed by the sobbing and crying of a girl.*

*Suddenly, a piercing scream rent the air, and then a sort of subdued scream and sigh as if she was being choked to stop her from screaming.*

*This was too much for all concerned as their nerves started to crack.*

The anonymous author of that anecdote further stated that each of the young persons who came back was willing to sign affidavits as to its veracity.

There is still another interesting legend from Port Clinton, this time taken from the pages of the *Schuylkill Haven Call* newspaper in its March 24, 1917 edition.

*Frozen solid in the ice in the dock at Port Clinton is the hat of William Glassmier, who November 24 last committed suicide by jumping into the waters off the dock.*

*For years, the people at Port Clinton have been cutting ice from the dock and storing it for consumption during summer months.*

*Now they refuse to cut it, believing the spirit of Glassmier still lingers in the frozen water, and when the ice melts, his spirit will venture forth to again walk the streets of the community.*

•

A story has been told about a large black dog that appeared to a group of boys walking along Seven Stars Road, north of **Schuylkill Haven**.

The dog seemed to come out of nowhere and approached the boys. As one of them leaned over to pet the dog–*poof!*–it vanished into thin air!

•

In the southwestern corner of Schuylkill County, near **Tower City**, is told the tale of a glowing ghost that treads a trail on the slope of Broad Mountain.

Just off Gold Mine Road at High Rocks, we were told, the spirit was once seen, and perhaps still roams.

"My grandfather told me a headless ghost used to wheel its head on a wheelbarrow up there," one local resident said. "We used to wait at night, and when it got dark you could see it going along the old railroad bed on the mountain. You'd see a flash of light every now and then. They said it was the ghost of an old miner who lost his head in a mine accident, and he was carrying his head in a wheelbarrow along the old railroad bed.

"My father told me it was probably just fireballs from 'ghost wood,' or rotting railroad ties. No matter what, it used to make the hairs on our necks stand up. We used to sit out there for hours and watch for it!"

•

Richard and Ellen DeFeo moved to **Jim Thorpe** in 1998 to pursue his retirement dream to operate a bed and breakfast inn.

They found a stunning ca. 1880 Queen Anne-style mansion at 5 West Broadway and converted it into the Manor at Opera House Square, a hauntingly charming B&B that also includes the Selective Eye antiques shop.

The phrase "hauntingly charming" was used intentionally, but the haunting of the Manor is a tad different from any you will read in this book.

Richard is a talented artist, designer, and teacher, and his touching story actually began when he composed the internet site for the B&B and added a bit of wit on the web site.

"I added that the Manor was a very safe place," he said, because we had a 'guard cat' named Larry."

Larry was one of three kittens that were "deposited" by a momma cat. The kittens were given the names "Larry, Darryl, and Darryl," after offbeat characters on a popular television show of the time. The Darryls were given away, but Larry became a fixture at the B&B.

"Nothing stopped Larry," DeFeo said. "He would go up to our Great Dane and nuzzle up to him. He was fearless."

Not even being struck by a car and injured fettered this feline. He quickly recovered and was back on "guard duty" in short order.

Web surfers would read the reference to Larry on the Manor's site, book a room, and upon arrival immediately ask where the "guard cat" was. Larry became a cult figure to the guests.

Sadly, Larry died in late 2003. But, if cats indeed have nine lives, Larry may have a tenth.

"Since his death, though, we have had a couple of, I guess you could say, 'sightings' of Larry," DeFeo said.

"Larry and I had a little ritual of the years. I would settle in to watch TV, put a blanket on my lap, and Larry would jump up and we'd watch TV together until he fell asleep on my belly.

"Another thing was that when we were away, we'd come home and Larry would hear us coming up the porch. We had an upholstered rocking chair that he wasn't allowed on because he shed too much hair.

"Well, we'd know that he was doing something he shouldn't have because as we came in the house, the rocker would be rocking because he had just jumped off of it.

"About a month after he died, we came home and I noticed that the rocker was moving as we entered. Now, he wasn't with us any longer, and there was nobody else in the house.

"That same thing would happen on two or three more occasions."

DeFeo tried to rationalize and find logical explanations for the rocking of the rocker, but could find none.

"After a while," he continued, "I gave it no more thought. Then, we had guests who were booked into the Blue Room. They came down in the morning and asked us about Larry.

"They told us they had seen him the previous night. They said they had cats at home and they slept with them in their bed. That night, the woman told us, she felt a kneading motion, as if a cat were there in the bed with them.

"Then, she said, she saw the outline and the image of a cat. When she identified the color and appearance of that image, it was the perfect description of Larry."

DeFeo had no reason not to believe the woman, who was quite serious about her sighting.

"From that point on," he said with emotion, "I changed the internet site copy to read 'The *spirit* of Larry still guards the Manor B&B.

"And, I truly believe it does!"

•

Coal Country is drenched with legends, traditions, and superstitions that were carried into it from the immigrants who flooded into Schuylkill, Carbon, and other anthracite region counties.

One of the eeriest of those beliefs is that of "Corpse Candles," which can be found in the folklore of Wales, Ireland, and England.

And, perhaps, in the Charles Baber Cemetery in **Pottsville**.

The late Ethel Manning, a popular and prominent Pottsville writer entrepreneur, wrote to this writer several years ago and related the experience of a group of boys who were playing baseball many years ago in a section of the cemetery grounds where burials had not yet taken place.

As darkness fell on their game, one of the boys pointed out a weird flickering in the distance–in the "old section" of the graveyard.

One by one, the boys affixed their eyes on the strange phenomenon. They clearly saw what they described as a glowing light, at about the height of a person's shoulders, bobbing gently along a path of the cemetery. It was also evident that nobody was there, holding the light.

Manning came to the conclusion that it may well have been a *canwyll corph*, the Welsh term for the light that is said to appear as a precursor of a death.

According to the legend, the candles represent the souls of the departed and are extinguished when those souls leave the earth.

In some sections of the British Isles, the lights are also harbingers of death and appear to those who are about to pass on.

The boys in the Baber Cemetery chose not to ponder the question–they saw enough of the mysterious lights and fled quickly.

And, happily, all lived to tell the story.

•

Although the resident preferred her name and address not be used, one fellow in **Pine Grove** told of a brief but shocking encounter that took place in her own back yard.

She was hanging wash, and had a feeling that someone was looking at her. She turned around and caught the fleeting glimpse of a woman, clad in a high-necked dress and with her hair in a bun. She fixed a gaze upon her for only a moment until she vanished.

Another Pine Grove resident, in another anonymous residence, said he regularly saw the spirit of a Civil War soldier in his basement, and eventually confirmed the existence of three ghosts in his otherwise pleasant home.

In Pine Grove is the bizarre story of a woman who died in childbirth and was buried in a small graveyard at the end of town. It is said that a few years later, the casket was to be moved to a large plot the family had purchased.

When the coffin was exhumed, it was somehow opened, and witnesses saw horrid scratch marks and bits of nail and flesh on the inside of the top of the coffin. The hapless woman had been buried alive! She was reinterred in the family plot at St. John's Lutheran cemetery in town.

•

**Girardville** resident Bruce Bitting recalled a somewhat personal experience with the unknown.

His father had built a home in the town, and he and Bruce's mother had lived there until the both passed away in the early 1990s.

"We rented the house out after my mother passed away," Bruce said. From the very start, he found a strange irony. His parents' names were Don and Mary, the renters' names were Dan and Marie.

"One day," he said, "Marie told us that she had heard giggling in the house when no one was there." The woman turned in response, and saw a woman standing in the doorway. She asked the woman who she was and why she was there, but the figure simply disappeared.

When the renter described the giggle and the woman, both he and other families agreed that who she heard and who she saw was likely his mother.

That, and another experience his own wife had in the house, has led Bruce to believe that the energies of his parents may remain in the house.

He had helped his father build a bathroom in the house. They had put much love and labor into the project. After his father died, Bruce's wife occasionally caught the aroma of Old Spice after shave lotion, the only kind Bruce's father would ever use.

•

A story has circulated for years about the ghost *woman* that glides through the graveyard of the ghost *town* of **Hickory Run**.

Once a thriving trading post, the village is survived only by a small chapel and a building that now serves as the office of Hickory Run State Park.

That village and nearby Saylorsville were consumed by a flood that swept them away when several dams broke in October, 1849. Seven people, including Lizzie West and her four children, ages one to 15, perished. Lizzie was the wife of the village blacksmith, Jacob West, who was not killed in the flood and lived another 27 years.

Some believe it is the ghost of mother Lizzie who rambles through the graveyard still today, searching forever, and for whatever.

•

There are times when in the course of collecting ghost stories that one feels as if they become privy to most private, intimate details of some peoples' lives, such as witnessed in the previous paragraphs.

The following is the text of the letter from a **Ringtown** man who felt compelled, for reasons known only to himself, to relate his very personal story. He responded after a newspaper printed an article about a talk this writer gave several years ago in Schuylkill County. Although it may seem trivial to some readers, they only have to put themselves in his place to understand why he took the time to write.

*Dear Mr. Adams:*

*From the Shenandoah Evening Herald: "In Pocono Ghosts," Adams explains that paranormal researchers believe the body emits a burst of energy at the time of a traumatic experience, such as a violent death. This energy, which he believes can't be destroyed, may be imprinted somehow at the site of the trauma."*

*This made me send for your book and also to say I think this is true. I would like to tell of something I experienced.*

*My wife died in February, 1988. Sometime between then and February, 1990: During the night I heard a bang against the wall of the bedroom. I heard my name called. I saw someone standing beside the bed.*

*So, I began to put down on paper the time and date things happened.*

*1/20/90, about two o'clock: A reflection from the mirror on the dresser.*

*2/20/90, midnight: A swish of air across the*

*foot end of the bed.*

*2/22/90, midnight: A rap on the wall.*

*2/22/90, morning:  A man with a hat at the window.*

*At the end of your Poconos book you asked for other experiences so I thought I would write.*

*Yours truly,*
*G.R.,*
*Ringtown, Pa.*

Again, this gentleman's story is not, in and of itself, frightening or even remarkable.

But, I have often been asked what I believe to be the most frightening ghost story I have ever investigated or heard.

I have been in places where mass murders were committed.  I have stayed in or visited some of the most legendary haunted castles, inns, and houses in America and Europe.  In the more than 20 years I have been collecting stories and investigating hauntings I have spoken with thousands of individuals who have had encounters and have had hundreds of my own.

Still, among the gory suicides, bloody ax-murders, and untold horrors, the scariest ghost stories of all are sometimes the simplest. That Ringtown man was obviously moved, and perhaps mortified by his visions and feelings.

The scariest ghost stories are those that are

experienced by the average man, woman, or child who was totally unprepared and unequipped to deal with them.

The majority of people who come forth with stories never once in their lives believed they would ever sense or see a ghost. Some said they never even believed in ghosts until one entered their lives. When they did, they were confused at first, and either confounded or comforted as they fully absorbed and understood the reality of what happened.

A line in the 2003 movie, "Pirates of the Caribbean" captured that quite succinctly.

The female lead character in the movie steadfastly stood her ground and maintained her conviction that ghosts do not exist, despite what was becoming insurmountable evidence that the pirate ship she was sailing on was a ghost ship crewed by the living dead.

At one climactic point, one very scary pirate stared at the woman and cackled, "Aye, lassie, ye better start believin' in ghost stories now...because you're in one!"

For me as the collector of ghost stories, and for anyone who has ever had their thoughts, and sometimes their lives, turned around by that first ghostly experience, that ghoulish buccaneer spoke volumes.

# AFTERWORD

We now come to the end of this book, but certainly not to the end of the quest for more stories of hauntings in Coal Country.

The unsurpassed courtesies and cooperation on the part of the people of Schuylkill and Carbon counties made the usually tedious phase of researching extraordinarily easy.

Ask about ghosts at the Pottsville Free Public Library and there's a file on the subject front-and-center at the reference desk. Ask about ghosts at the Schuylkill County Visitors Center and its director provides a list of contact names and story leads from the top of his head.

Regrettably, time and page count restrictions resulted in too many contacts not made, leads not followed, and stories left undiscovered.

This region–this "Coal Country"–is steeped in history that its people hold dear to their hearts. In the villages and valleys, the cities and towns of Schuylkill and Carbon counties are many more tales to be told.

A "Coal Country Ghosts: Book Two." story file has already been established. Should you care to add to it, we invite you to write to Exeter House Books, PO Box 8134, Reading, PA 19603 or email *Stories@ExeterHouseBooks.com*.

*Charles J. Adams III, 2004*